Four Square Miles

the circumstance

Four Square Miles

A story of pride, love, family, and a dream.

KEITH MICHAEL PRESTON

Copyright © 2020 by Keith Michael Preston

ISBN: 978-1-7345925-1-1

Cover Art Designed by Thomas J. Zaffo/B. DeAngelo

Typesetting & Layout by Monte Press Inc.

Printed in the U.S.A.

I am forever grateful to my spouse, Nancy Preston, my mother, Diane Preston, and father, George Preston for their continued support.

I would like to show appreciation to the following individuals for their invaluable advice and ongoing support while creating this book: Caroline Adams, Annette Nasti-Coppola, Marie Miserendino, and Amy Corcoran.

FOUR SQUARE MILES is a series that
takes place in a suburb of New York City.

the circumstance is the second of the series.

CHAPTER 1

It's approximately 11:30pm and Nutsy and Ladro are wrapping up their conversation in Nutsy's kitchen after polishing off a bottle of scotch. It was a long night and Nutsy had to make important decisions with his right-hand man.

Kathy's upstairs steaming while pacing in the hallway after overhearing Nutsy's final decision regarding his group's proposal. Well, let's say it is more of a shakedown and Nutsy wants no part of it.

Although Kathy knows her husband's group deliberately backed him up against a wall, she still wants Nutsy to take the safe way by accepting their proposal and giving up some of his profits. The group is comprised of four surrounding bookies. Nutsy controls The Vern, Squalo is the main bookie of The Plains, Belo controls The Hills, and Donnola controls New Row.

Squalo, Bello, and Donnola have seen profits in their areas steadily decline while Nutsy's sports gambling business in The Vern, a densely populated city, has been flourishing. They have become envious of Nutsy's success and want him to share his profits with them. They are threatening not to accept any of his future layoff bets if he doesn't cooperate.

It's late but Kathy still dials her cell phone and impatiently waits for her father to answer. Her father has been away at an exotic beach front resort and is currently sitting at a pool bar having drinks with a few ladies.

Billy notices his cell phone ringing and immediately thinks something is not right because of the time so he nervously answers, "What's wrong?"

"I hate to ask you to cut your vacation short, but I overheard Nutsy's decision."

"Oh... I've been expecting this."

"What do you mean, oh?" Kathy nervously asks.

"I thought it was something else."

"Did you hear me? Nutsy's not taking the offer."

"Like I said, I was expecting this. I'll get back as soon as I can. Hang in there." Billy hangs up and says to the bartender, "Make it a double this time. It looks like it's my last night."

While Nutsy and Ladro now stand by the front door and exchange a handshake, Nutsy says, "I meant to ask ya. Are ya startin' to take that shit again for your leg?"

"A little bit here and there, why?"

"Ya screwed up the teaser bet with Munchie."

"The Doc? How?"

Nutsy pulls out a slip of paper from his pants pocket and replies, "Well first off, both of ya thought he pushed giving five which is wrong. But you're scrambling the numbers again."

"What did I do?"

Nutsy scans the paper and replies, "Your slip says, plus five, minus six for minus one. It should've been, minus five, plus six for plus one."

"Minus one, plus one, it's close enough."

"I told ya to lay off that shit. It gives ya dyslexia or something."

"Oh well, he thought he pushed with the five-point spread anyway… fuck him for not doing his own homework."

Nutsy laughs and replies, "Nah, we gotta make good. Am I gonna have to check all your slips now?"

"Well, it looks like you have been already. Besides, I think it's the computers. The numbers don't look the same to me."

"A five is a five, isn't it?"

"It's like a book reader who only reads books because the words look different on that, ah… what's that shit they read on?"

"What are ya talkin' about, a Kindle?"

"Yeah, that's it. I've been married to your sister for years and she still pays ten times more to read a book because the computer messes with her eyes."

"That's different. You're scrambling the six points. I think it's time we all do a refresher course."

Kathy leans her head out of the second story window and whispers, "You're both talking too loud."

Nutsy replies, "We're sayin' goodbye."

"Well, hurry up." Kathy leans back in.

"What are we, realtors and insurance agents now?" Ladro asks.

"It can't hurt. Plus, these new young guys look fuckin' lost."

"Isn't that the truth?" Ladro turns and stumbles down the blue-stone walkway toward his car that is parked on the street.

Nutsy notices and says, "Maybe you should walk home."

"I used to drive worse than this when I snuck the car out when I was fifteen, remember?"

"Who can forget that?"

Ladro pauses and turns. "Remember that time I had like ten people piled in the car and we drove all night doing donuts down the street in the snow?"

"Yeah, good thing Billy knew the cop that pulled us over. The inside of the car was smokier than the Halen concert we saw in the 80s."

Ladro laughs and replies, "Shit, his eyes popped out when I opened the window. Time seemed so simple back then, ha, Nutsy?"

"We didn't realize how good we had it. All we –"

Kathy leans her head out of the window again and whispers, "Will you two knock it off. You're going to wake up the neighbors."

"I'll see ya tomorrow," Nutsy says to Ladro.

Ladro raises his arm up to say goodnight and stumbles away.

Nutsy stumbles back into his house and then attempts to step up the staircase. He's taking it slow, step by step.

Kathy stands in the hallway waiting for him with a pissed off look. "What are ya still doing up?" Nutsy asks.

Kathy replies, "You'll never learn, will you?"

Nutsy finally makes it to the top step and stumbles down the hallway. "Learn what?"

"This group's playing you for a fool. Don't you think Squalo already knows you'll never bow down?"

Nutsy pauses and braces himself against a wall. "I'm not gonna explain my decision. And ya shouldn't be eaves droppin' on my conversation."

"How could I not? You and Ladro sound like baffling idiots, downstairs. The lion this, the lion that. You should only hear yourselves. You sound like morons."

Sammy peeks out of her bedroom door and says, "Dad, I need two hundred dollars for the house deposit."

"What house deposit?"

Kathy replies, "I told you already. Her friend reserved a house down at Seaside for graduation weekend."

"Ya never told me that… she can go for the day and I'll pick her up at night."

While Sammy glances at Nutsy with an annoyed look, Kathy replies, "They're staying for the weekend."

"The weekend? Fuck that!" Nutsy replies.

Sammy replies, "Mom already said it was alright."

"Is that right? Nutsy glances toward Kathy and asks, "You're making all the decisions now?"

"Not the important ones, I can see." Kathy says to Sammy, "I'll give you the money in the morning."

Sammy nods and closes her bedroom door.

"What the hell is this all about?" Nutsy asks.

"Stop acting surprised. You came down with me when I graduated, remember?"

They both enter their bedroom and Nutsy slips off his shirt. For an older man, he's in decent shape. A nasty scar runs down his right shoulder.

"Yeah, and ya stayed in the room with your father all night."

"Nutsy, that was a hundred years ago. Times are different."

"Yeah, times are times. Times are different. That's all everyone says now… it's all bullshit."

"Don't change the topic."

Nutsy plops on the edge of the bed and removes his watch. "You'll never understand anyway."

"Try me."

"I work in a jungle with lions and tigers. Once I lay down, I'll be eaten alive."

"Jesus Christ! When are you going to get over this?"

Nutsy's voice gets a little louder. "Over what?"

"You're fifty now. Who cares if you give up a little? We'll still be comfortable."

"I do… and it's my business."

Kathy moves away and says, "The lions and tigers are the least of your worries because you're going to eat yourself alive before they do. And they already know that."

"Ya know who ya married. It was never a secret."

Kathy replies from the bathroom, "Yeah, you're right, a lion who still thinks like a cub. Just go to sleep. You look like a mess."

"How about a little action first?"

"Sure, go see Suzie palm."

Nutsy can't help but laugh.

CHAPTER 2

Ladro stumbles into his house and is confronted by Blackie in the foyer who is now annoyed after hearing the news from Kathy. "How much did you drink?" Blackie asks.

"Your brother and I had to discuss a few important things."

"This is how you drove home? Are you crazy? You already totaled a car like this."

"I'm fine."

"You're not fine and you're egging him on, you know that."

"Nutsy doesn't like eggs."

"Don't mess with me. I'm not in the mood. You know how to push his buttons."

"What are you talking about? Nutsy's a grown man. If anything, he pushes my buttons."

"Bullshit. I heard about your conversation." Blackie sarcastically continues on, "We only need six friends in the end. That ain't the Nutsy I know. What the hell is that shit about?"

Ladro can't help but laugh.

Blackie continues on, "Go ahead, laugh. This group's gonna flush you both down the drain. You're supposed to be his main guy. Start acting like it."

The next morning, Nutsy sits at the island slurping down his coffee with a splitting headache. Billy is arriving home from vacation soon and Nutsy has a feeling that Kathy already told her father about his decision.

Nutsy has always been respectful of his father-in-law and is concerned their conversation could get out of hand since he knows Billy is on Kathy's side.

Kathy wanders in and opens the pantry door without speaking a word. Nutsy peers over toward her and thinks she's purposely ignoring him, and he's right.

Although Kathy usually joins Nutsy at the island for breakfast, she decides to sit at the table by herself. She still hasn't glanced his way, so Nutsy just remains silent and slurps his coffee again.

Nutsy pours Captain into a bowl and then fills the bowl with milk. Kathy finally looks over and says, "Make sure you clean up your mess. The maid is off duty."

"What was this shit about Seaside last night?"

The doorbell rings and Kathy says, "We went over it already. Just sit and let the lion relax. I'll get it." Kathy races out of the kitchen.

Nutsy mumbles under his breath, "Wise-ass."

Kathy opens the front door and Ladro steps in and gives Kathy a kiss on the cheek. She can smell the booze on him too. So Kathy heads back toward the kitchen and says, "You smell worse than your friend this morning."

Ladro already got hammered by Blackie all night so he remains silent. He can tell by Kathy's tone she is annoyed.

They both enter the kitchen and Kathy sarcastically says, "I'll make sure I buy extra meat tonight, so the lion eats well since it might be your last meal." Kathy grabs her bag off the counter and races out.

Ladro takes a seat at the island and says, "She doesn't seem happy right now."

Nutsy nods and replies, "I heard it all fuckin' night. I think I slept two hours."

"Yeah, believe me. Blackie ain't thrilled either. I guess Kathy called her." Ladro whips out his cell phone and looks at the screen. "Check this out. The Crew is coming to Citi."

"I thought they retired?"

"Yeah, for the tenth time already. It's easy money for them now. You wanna go?"

"We saw them like, four times already... oh, before I forget, Tiffany got us in the Wall Street pool."

"The big one?"

"Yup... a mill payout, imagine hittin' that thing?"

"Yeah sure, these hedge fund crooks probably have it fixed already."

Meanwhile, Munchie and Belinda are currently in bed at Belinda's apartment. While Munchie thrusts back and forth on top of her, Belinda's eyes roll and she asks, "Are you ever gonna get it up?"

Munchie pauses and replies, "I'm almost there."

"Almost where? You said the same thing ten minutes ago. Just get off me now."

Ladro notices the box of Captain on the island and asks, "You still eat this shit?"

"Shit? It's the best."

"Sure, if you want your teeth to fall out."

Sammy yells from the top of the stairway. "Dad, don't forget to leave the Seaside deposit!"

"I thought your mother gave it to you!" Nutsy yells back.

"She forgot! Just leave it on the counter if you go out!" Sammy replies.

Nutsy glances toward Ladro and whispers, "What a bunch of bullshit."

Ladro laughs and asks, "The seniors still go down there?"

"Yeah, I guess so."

"Man, was I hammered all weekend."

"That's what I'm talkin' about… and there's a lot of creeps out there today."

"Just talk to her."

"She won't listen to shit anyway."

"She's a teenager, Nutsy. Did we listen at her age?"

"But we knew more than our parents did."

Ladro laughs and asks, "Do you hear yourself?"

CHAPTER 3

Blackie drives her black BMW and Kathy sits in the passenger seat heading to a lunch for Belo's wife, Linda. Ten ladies meet up for each other's birthday during the year at random restaurants throughout the county.

Kathy and Blackie are not crazy about going but decided it wasn't Linda's decision to go against Nutsy and shouldn't hold it against her.

Somehow, they hope to tell Linda what is happening if she doesn't already know. Kathy says with an annoyed tone, "Lions. Who the hell do they think they are?"

Blackie replies, "There's only one lion, and he's locked up for good."

"We can only hope so."

"I'm pissed off at Ladro. He knows he pushes Nutsy's buttons."

"It's not his fault. Your brother's as stubborn as they come."

"Oh, I know that. Trust me, Ladro's no slouch either. They're made for each other."

Meanwhile, Nutsy and Ladro are now heading down a long hallway in a commercial building on 1st Street. They are on the way to meet their accountant and lawyer to discuss a situation regarding the sales tax at Sista.

Marcus is the attorney and Staci is the accountant and they are twins. Nutsy and Ladro have known them forever and they handle all their tax and legal matters. Plus, they're also top players in the political party with Billy.

Nutsy and Ladro stroll into their conference room where Marcus and Staci are both present and Nutsy sarcastically says, "One sues 'em and the other screws 'em."

Staci replies, "Keep talking that way and I'll let you deal with the sales tax guy yourself."

"I always loved your sense of humor, Staci."

They all exchange a handshake and take a seat. "What does this dipshit want now?" Nutsy asks.

Staci replies, "He said your numbers don't add up."

Nutsy replies, "Well maybe, this clown can't add."

Marcus laughs and replies, "She's talking about what you report. He said Sista does more volume than what you say."

"I gotta tell ya, they should spend more time cleaning this state up than busting all the owners… ya know what."

Staci laughs and replies, "Yeah, we know… he wants the number higher or he's going to start poking around."

"By how much are we talkin' about?"

"Another fifteen grand," Staci replies.

"Screw that... these guys are the biggest crooks around. All they do is squeeze the shit out of businesses."

Marcus replies, "I understand, but the sales tax department marches to a different drum. If you don't agree, they'll start looking into your personal items."

"No wonder ya see everyone bailing out of this state. They're tired of these shakedown artists."

Staci asks, "What do you want me to tell him?"

"Can I beat it?" Nutsy asks.

"Maybe, as long as you can justify it one hundred percent."

So Nutsy leans back and crosses his arms. As he catches eyes with Ladro who shakes his head no, Nutsy hesitantly replies, "It seems like I don't have too much of a choice, now does it?"

"Looking at Ladro, I guess not... on a different note, have you given any thought to what I asked you?"

Nutsy replies, "Ya know me, Staci, I've never been much of a political person."

Marcus replies, "Are you kidding? You're at every fundraiser with four, five tables. You donate, help the Little League, what do you call that?"

"I'm a behind the scenes guy. Always been and always will be."

Staci replies, "I'll still never forget that speech you made when Billy asked you to say a few words at the Club."

"Yeah, I can't believe he did that to me."

"Do you remember what you said?" Staci asks.

"I said a lot that night."

"Well, I didn't forget. You said, 'The eyes tell if a person's soul is good, not their color, race, or religion. What's deep inside a person, is what counts in the end.'

"It's the truth... I'm Italian and they're the ones tryin' to screw me over right now."

Marcus replies, "This is what Staci is trying to say. You take people for who they are, not what they are. Let's face it, if that wasn't the case, I wouldn't be your attorney and Staci wouldn't be your accountant."

"Our fathers were friends. When mine passed away yours made it his business to check on me. Besides, me gettin' involved with the party would never work. Everyone knows what I do."

"They don't care what you do, they care who you are. You've always been a voice of reason and good for this city," Staci says.

"That's Billy's job anyway, he loves being involved in the political game, I don't."

"Just think it over again," Staci says.

As Nutsy nods, Marcus asks, "So I heard Tiffany got you in the Wall Street pool?"

"Yeah, if I hit, I'll buy the sales tax crook a nice gift."

Staci laughs and says, "I'm sure you will." She leans over and picks up two presents off the floor and places them in front of Nutsy.

"What's this?" Nutsy asks.

"We have to travel out of town and can't make the party. They're for your son and mother."

After the meeting with their lawyer and accountant, Nutsy and Ladro stop back at Nutsy's house since Nutsy forgot some wager slips.

Sammy wanders into the kitchen and says, "Hey, Uncle Larry." She gives him a kiss on the cheek. Not many people call him Larry but it's what Sammy's been used to since she was a kid. His full name is Lawrence Tisi.

"Don't you have school?" Ladro asks.

"My next two periods were cancelled."

Nutsy strolls in and overhears Sammy's comment and replies, "That's the oldest trick in the book."

Sammy asks, "Don't you ever trust anyone?"

"Not really."

Ladro laughs and asks, "Are you working out later with your aunt?"

Sammy glances toward Nutsy. At this point, Nutsy knew nothing about Blackie training Sammy with karate techniques. "What's he talkin' about?" Nutsy asks Sammy.

Ladro had no idea Nutsy didn't know so he says, "I'm sorry, Sammy."

"It's okay. I'm a big girl now." Sammy glances at Nutsy and says, "I've been training with Aunt Blackie."

"Is that so?"

"Yup, I have to go." Sammy gives Nutsy and Ladro a peck on the cheek and moves away but pauses. "Oh, you didn't leave the deposit this morning."

While Nutsy gives Sammy a look and remains silent, Sammy rolls her eyes and asks, "You're going to give me a hard time again, right?"

Nutsy reluctantly yanks out a roll of cash from his pants pocket and sorts through it. He holds out two, one-hundred-dollar bills. Sammy takes it and says, "Thank you!" She gives him another peck on the cheek and walks out.

Ladro says, "It seems like you two are getting along better."

"Yeah, it's because she needs money. Come back later." After the front door closes, Nutsy asks, "Ya fuckin' knew this and didn't tell me?"

"Nutsy, Blackie's just trying to help Sammy chase her dream."

"Being a Navy Seal ain't a dream. It's a death wish."

"We all have a death wish one way or another, don't we? I always wanted to be a gym teacher and I became a thief. Go figure."

"Gym teacher? Where the hell did this come from?"

"Yeah, imagine that… my parents wouldn't pay for college and then I got mixed up with the other nine thieves. Once we ran through Harlem like a steam roller. I said fuck it. What do I need college for?"

"Don't change the subject."

"I don't know, Nutsy. You know them two. They'd take on the world if they could."

CHAPTER 4

Blackie parks her car in a parking lot in front of an upscale Italian Restaurant in The Hills area and asks Kathy, "Are you going to say anything to Linda?"

"We'll see how it goes first."

They both enter the restaurant and exchange hugs and kisses with the ladies. Kathy hands Linda a wrapped present and says, "Happy birthday, Linda. This is from the both of us."

Linda gives Kathy a kiss and then hugs Blackie. "You still look great, Blackie. We should all have your genes."

"You're not looking too bad yourself," Blackie replies.

"So, how's Nutsy and Ladro been?"

While Kathy and Blackie peek toward each other and remain quiet, Linda notices their hesitation and asks, "What is it?"

Kathy replies, "I don't want to get into it here, Linda. It's your day."

"We've been friends forever. If there's a problem, I want to know."

Blackie shrugs and replies, "Go ahead. Tell her then."

Kathy hesitantly says, "Your husband and the other two seem to be making a move on Nutsy."

Linda asks, "What move?"

"I don't know all the details, but it sounds like if he doesn't accept their offer, they're pushing him out of the group."

"What?!"

Both Kathy and Blackie nod.

Later that afternoon in The Hills section, Belo is in his office on Central Park Avenue writing down his totals for the day when Linda storms in and asks, "You're trying to screw Nutsy now?"

Belo knew this would eventually get back to Linda, so he hesitantly says, "We're all taking a hit except him, Linda. What would you expect us to do?"

"You're siding with the wrong two. They're both assholes and you know it... how could you even think about doing this?"

Down deep inside, Belo knows she's right. This has been eating away at him for days, but he won't let anyone know and keeps it to himself.

Linda continues, "No wonder you haven't been eating, and shitting diarrhea every night."

"It's only business. This is how things go sometimes."

"Who was the one who stood up for you when you played baseball, huh? All the times the other players broke your balls because you're a mulatto. Who? Who was it?" Linda's voice gets louder. "It was Nutsy, that's who! He didn't care because he considered you a friend!"

"You don't understand and never will."

Linda presses on, "I don't care what I understand. Lick his balls if you have to, but make this right with Nutsy. I felt like an asshole in front of them today."

Linda storms away and Belo sighs. Linda turns and says, "And another thing, that issue at the bar that Bono was at the other night, he was with Sammy. Did you know that?"

"Sammy? What the hell are you talking about?"

"Apparently, they met at a recruitment center and became friends."

"I did your brother a favor and brought Bono up from the shit hole south and now this?"

"This is my nephew we're talking about. Just make it right with Nutsy." Linda storms away.

Belo's eyes close.

After school was over, Sammy and a few girlfriends stroll down Grand Street heading home. It's a one-way street a block away from a parkway and runs east and west in the city.

They are all excitingly discussing their graduation weekend at Seaside and what events they can attend. It's an exciting time for them all.

The busted up van from Belinda's body shop skids right near them and Vito blurts out of the driver's side window, "I knew I'd run into ya sooner or later."

Sammy's girlfriends all nervously gather closer to one another as Sammy replies, "Just get lost. I got in enough trouble the other night."

The man sitting in the passenger seat has a bruised face. He was the one who smashed his nose on the dashboard the other night when Vito had angrily slammed on the brakes. The man says, "Stop playing around. We don't have time for this shit. Let's go."

Vito ignores him and rolls the truck slowly along the side of the nervous girls. "We'll meet up again one night, I'm sure."

Sammy sarcastically replies, "Great. I look forward to it."

"Maybe next time that wimp can fight his own battles."

"This has nothing to do with Bono now."

"It sure does."

Sammy has to break balls now. "By the way, how's your neck been feeling?"

While the man in the passenger seat breaks out in laughter, Vito glares toward him and asks, "What the fuck are you laughing at?"

"That was great," the man replies while trying to hold back his laughter.

"Ya think so?" Vito asks with an annoyed look.

"We have ten more cars to find and you're screwing around. Just hit the fucking pedal already."

Vito glances out of the window and says, "I'll see ya around." Vito slams on the gas and the truck peels out.

One of Sammy's friends asks her, "You know that asshole?"

"Unfortunately," Sammy replies.

The truck flies down the street and then bounces off of a parked car about a quarter of a mile ahead.

One of Sammy's friends asks, "Did you see that idiot?"

"He's probably still dizzy from the time I flipped him over," Sammy laughs.

CHAPTER 5

Meanwhile, Squalo is at one of the New York State jails sitting behind a glass partition having a conversation with his son, Leo. Leo was the original founder of The Lincoln Lords and owns the body shop that Belinda currently runs. About ten years ago, he was busted for running narcotics and illegal arms out of the store.

At the same time Squalo was the top bookie in The Vern. They were both bad for business especially for the big contractors investing into large city projects. It was during a similar time like today, when big money was being invested in city development.

All these years while Leo was away and Squalo moved out of town, Nutsy helped keep The Vern somewhat clean. Although he ran his gambling operation, he always frowned upon narcotics and arms dealing.

The big players respected that about Nutsy and Billy always made sure Nutsy stayed on that path. The time years back when Nutsy got hit for big money tempted him to dabble in narcotics, but he couldn't live with himself knowing he was putting that garbage on the streets. After all, he had two young children of his own at that time.

Leo has slicked back dark hair and piercing round eyes. He is definitely someone you wouldn't want your daughter to marry, or even date for that matter.

He has a bunch of slash marks across one cheek making him look like the career criminal that he is. His muscular body and tattoos add to his rough, intimidating appearance.

From behind the glass partition Leo says, "I gotta good feeling. The new laws might do it this time."

"Just hurry up. I already stuck Nutsy in a corner."

"Did you tell anyone I got a shot?"

"No one knows a thing."

"I'm sure Billy might know."

"Nah, they all think you got at least another ten to go."

"Did that weasel, Donnola ever get married?"

"Who the fuck would marry that rodent?"

Leo laughs and replies, "What about the shop and the group?"

"Well hopefully, you'll get the fuck outta here and take it back over."

"What about Belinda?"

"Your sister's a tough girl but never had the killer instinct you do. She'll never be able to handle what could come down."

"Is the Quad still intact?"

"That I don't know. They keep it close to the vest."

A security guard yells out, "Leo! Time's up!"

Leo doesn't respond to the officer and asks Squalo, "You know it was them, right?"

The guard yells out, "I'm not gonna say it again!"

Squalo stands up and says, "Go. You don't need any issues right now. Just do what you gotta to get out."

Billy was able to find a flight the next day and took it back home. He decided to stop by Kathy's house first since she seemed nervous on the phone and he wanted to check on their situation.

Billy rings her doorbell and waits. He looks relaxed with a deep tan and white hair neatly combed. Kathy finally opens the door and gives Billy a hug. "Wow, you look great, dad."

Billy whispers, "Is he here?" Kathy nods and they both stroll into the kitchen where Nutsy is sipping his coffee by the island. Nutsy notices Billy and immediately gets nervous since he wasn't expecting Billy to arrive home for at least a few more days.

"How come you're home so early?" Nutsy asks.

"How much tanning and eating can a man do? Besides, I was getting bored."

Nutsy knows this is bullshit. Billy goes away often and has never left a vacation early like this. Nutsy's expecting Billy to lay it in on him, so he tries to divert his attention. "Look at you. Ya should be on the cover of a modeling magazine."

Nutsy stands up and exchanges a handshake with Billy. "Yeah sure," Billy replies.

Billy gives Kathy a nod to leave the room and she says, "I have to go to the store. I'll be back in a little while."

Billy takes a seat at the island and pours himself a cup of coffee. Nutsy's surprised that Billy hasn't stormed in yelling and screaming. Maybe, the vacation relaxed him, Nutsy thinks.

So they both sit and slurp their coffee without a word for a moment. Billy is an incredibly patient man. No one will ever know if he's rattled or not and he has tried to calm Nutsy down over the years. It's helped a lot but Nutsy can still blow a fuse once in a while.

Billy starts off the conversation and asks, "How does your mother like it down south?"

Nutsy can't believe this is how their conversation has started. Maybe he doesn't know anything, Nutsy thinks. So Nutsy replies, "She loves it. She plays pinochle all day."

"Yeah, I'm sure. I'm starting to enjoy the warmer weather a little more myself. Maybe I'll go visit her one day and check it out."

All Nutsy can think about is, did this guy fall in love or something on vacation? So Nutsy replies, "She'd love that. Ya gotta eat a lot of protein to keep up with her though."

While Nutsy laughs, Billy sips his coffee and nonchalantly asks, "Do you remember a long time ago when Kathy brought you into the private room when I was at dinner with a bunch of people?"

"If it's the time I'm thinkin', I'd say that bunch of people ran the city."

Billy replies, "That's not what I asked you."

Nutsy has a feeling something is coming and replies, "Of course I remember. It was when we first started dating."

"And then you sat down and joined us, remember?"

"Yup. It was probably the most nerve-wracking night of my life."

"I'm sure it was. What were you like sixteen, seventeen?"

"I think I just turned seventeen." Nutsy has no idea where Billy's heading with this but knows it's leading somewhere.

"You sat and listened to everything everyone was saying and took it all in like a sponge."

"What was I supposed to do? I barely knew ya and you were with very important people that night."

"I was thinking to myself, this young man's sharp and knows how to handle himself. While you sat there and listened, you made ME do all the talking that night instead of me making YOU do all the talking. You played me good that night, Nutsy."

Nutsy replies, "Come on, I didn't play anyone."

Billy replies with a smile, "You sure did. Even some of the others at the table were impressed. That's why they eventually voted you in."

Nutsy's somewhat confused and asks, "What do ya mean by, voted me in?"

"That's for a later conversation… you're a sharp man, Nutsy. You've always been, but your emotions are now controlling your thoughts."

Nutsy now knows where this is heading and starts to reply but Billy cuts him off. "Did I finish? It's great to have pride but it's a stupid emotion that has taken down many men. Some strong, powerful, generous, just like you. But their pride fucking crippled them so badly that they became little boys again."

"Billy, I think you're getting –"

"Getting what, huh? Why, it can't happen to you? I'll accept whatever way you go, but that doesn't mean I have to agree with your decision… and I don't."

"Billy, there's more to it than just that."

"I've witnessed Squalo take down the best for many years by patiently watching as their pride and emotions ate themselves alive. There's no one better than him and he's doing it to you right now."

"I think you're givin' him more credit than he deserves."

"Don't be a fool, Nutsy. He backed you into a corner purposely knowing how you are... personally, I think he has more up his sleeve than just this."

"Like what?"

"I don't know, I just feel it. Take the deal and get the fuck out altogether, like I've been telling you all these years."

"Dad, we went over this already. I'm a high school dropout. It ain't like I can get a job at an accounting office or somethin' like that."

"You really think companies give a shit about that?"

"I got an idea. I can put down, experience, a street bookie for the past thirty years."

"Don't be a wise-ass. You never told me what it is, but this dream of yours, is it legal?"

As Nutsy nods, Billy asks, "It's about N-J, isn't it?"

Nutsy replies, "It couldn't happen anyway."

"Just imagine if Walt said that? If Edison, if Doubleday? Their dreams wouldn't be a reality today."

"I made my decision already."

"What do you think, I didn't know which way you were leaning? I'm not going to be around forever, but I'll promise you one thing, if you wanna chase your dream, I'll make sure it happens and you know I can do it."

Nutsy stays silent.

Billy continues on, "But you gotta be willing to eventually walk away."

"What is it with you? Why do you want me out so bad?"

Billy has his own personal reasons for wanting Nutsy to get out, but he says, "Don't take this the wrong way. You're a successful man, but you got more to offer in life, Nutsy."

CHAPTER 6

Meanwhile, Blackie and Ladro are in a heated discussion while pacing back and forth in their kitchen and Blackie says, "I want you to back off my brother."

Ladro asks, "Back off what?"

"He listens to you. Why? I don't know, but he does."

"What the fuck is that supposed to mean?"

"Just remember one thing, if he goes down, so will you." Blackie glances around. "My lousy salary at the bank isn't paying for all this."

"Just get me a key to the vault."

"Why is everything always a joke with you?"

"I'm not joking."

"Yeah, I wonder if your brother would ask for a do-over."

"That was fucking low," Ladro replies with an annoyed look.

"Nutsy's not thinking straight right now. You're leading him into the lion's cage, just like you led your brother."

Nutsy decides to take a trip to the sports park. While he leans his elbows on the same rusty fence as he always does, he gazes at the abandoned field in thought.

As his mind wanders back and forth, he can't help but think of his dream and whispers to himself, "This would take care of everything. Too bad it could never happen."

It's about an hour later and Nutsy has lost track of time. Although he made a final decision about his group, he's still somewhat torn. What if Billy's right? What if he can really make this happen? Nah, but it's just impossible. No one will take me serious enough.

As Nutsy's mind wavers back and forth, Ladro approaches him and says, "I've been trying to call you, but it keeps on going to voicemail."

Nutsy replies, "I turned it off. How'd ya know I was here?"

"If you're not at home, Sista, or N-J's, it's here. You're not too hard to figure out."

Ladro leans up against the fence and stares at the field. "This is it, ha, Nutsy?"

"Yup."

"What are you thinking, condos, attached houses?"

"Let's go." Nutsy turns and strolls away.

"What the fuck, Nutsy. If it ain't happening, just say it."

Nutsy replies while strolling toward the street, "Everyone will think I'm nuts anyway. Come on."

The same afternoon, Belinda and Squalo sit at a table having an early dinner at her tavern. Squalo has been toying with how to break the important news to Belinda that she will definitely not care for.

This news could change the whole dimension for Squalo's agenda toward Nutsy and could give him a real edge. Although he loves his daughter, he always felt she wasn't forceful enough while making decisions. Squalo always loved the aggressiveness of his son and how he violently handled matters.

So Squalo brings up Vito's situation first. "Tell me about this new kid."

"He has a lot to learn. He runs around like a punk all the time."

"Yeah, he'll never last anyway. Someone will eat him alive." Squalo already likes Vito but doesn't want to let on. He reminds him of his son while starting out.

"I try to tell him that, but he doesn't listen," Belinda replies.

"Just get rid of him then."

"He's a good earner though. He might be a wise-ass, but he hustles."

Squalo hesitates and then changes the conversation. "Your brother has a shot to get out."

"What!" Belinda replies with an annoyed look. She never had a good relationship with Leo. He always treated her like garbage, and in a way, turned her into the rough person she currently is. She never wanted this life but was forced into it by Leo.

Leo is the complete opposite of Nutsy. He did everything he could to suck Belinda into that life, whereas Nutsy did everything to get Blackie out.

"Don't look so thrilled," Squalo says.

"He can rot for all I care… I'm not taking him back in the shop. So don't ask me to."

"Taking him back? It was his shop and group before you took it over, remember?"

"What are you saying?"

"I think you can read between the lines."

After leaving the sports park, Nutsy decides to stop by Munchie's office. Nutsy takes a seat in one of the examining rooms while Munchie strolls in and asks, "Did you check it?"

So Nutsy whips out four-eighty rolled up from his jacket pocket and replies, "You were right. His slip was screwed up. Ya didn't push with the teaser."

Munchie takes the cash and replies, "I thought so. You didn't tell Ladro I called you, right?"

"No, and I don't want him to know either."

"How come you didn't notice this before?"

"I just get the wager and outcome. I don't see all the lines... don't ya keep track of your own bets?"

"I don't know, Nutsy, my mind's all screwed up right now."

"What's wrong?"

"Ah, just work stuff."

"Let me ask ya something. Are ya givin' Ladro that shit for his leg again?"

"You know I can't say anything, Nutsy."

So Nutsy hesitantly replies, "Take some time off. You're startin' to look like shit." Nutsy pats Munchie on the shoulder and moves away.

"Nutsy."

Nutsy turns. "What is it?"

"Thanks for being up-front."

Nutsy nods and walks out.

About a half an hour later, Nutsy strolls into The Headquarters to round up the workers. He wants to be certain everyone is clear with the details of the apparent fixed game.

As Nutsy moves behind the bar, he yells out, "Alright, I need everyone to listen up! The over and under on the Bears / Packers this weekend opened up at thirty-six!"

A man replies, "Thirty-six, that seems low for those two teams."

Nutsy replies, "Yeah, expect everyone to take the under on it."

The man asks, "Who would take the under with the line so low?"

Ladro replies while sitting on the couch, "Just be ready. If it becomes too lopsided one way, we need to know."

Another worker asks, "Why, you're really expecting suckers to take the under with such a low line?"

Nutsy replies, "Yup, and one last thing. If anyone wants to bet over a thousand times on this game, they need to pay up-front."

The man replies, "But we never collected up-front."

"Well, on this game we are. Don't walk in here with a ticket without the cash. I ain't bookin' it."

The over and under line is the total points on a game. If a gambler thinks the score will be high, they bet the over, and under if they think low. A low line would tempt bettors to take the over, but with a rumor of a locked bet, it wouldn't matter.

Most bettors will wager on a lock just for the hell of it. It would be like a rumor of lotto numbers being a given. People would play just so they wouldn't have any regrets if the rumor was correct, so Nutsy's expecting heavy wagers on this game.

He decided to collect up-front to prevent bettors from purposely calling in large wagers. He figured now they could only call in wagers of cash that they currently have in hand.

CHAPTER 7

Meanwhile, Kathy and Billy are on their way to visit N-J at the facility where he lives. When Billy's around he spends as much time with N-J as possible. Billy has a fabulous relationship with his grandson and cherishes their time together. He accepts N-J for who he is and always thought there was a reason for his autism. He truly believes N-J is special.

Kathy, on the other hand, occasionally questions how this could have happened. She doesn't discuss the topic with Nutsy but does bring it up from time to time with her father.

Billy is a positive and reassuring man. He would never allow Kathy to think it was something she could have prevented, or that it was her fault.

Kathy parks her car in the facility parking lot and they both slip out of the car. While strolling toward the front door, Billy says, "I can't believe N-J is turning twenty-one."

"You're telling me."

"Look, I know Carmela is turning seventy, but I want this birthday to be special for N-J. He deserves it, Kathy."

"I know he does. I'm sure she'll think so too."

They both enter the front door and walk down the hallway toward a room where N-J usually hangs out and plays with the other kids. When they get to N-J's room he immediately charges over yelling, "Grandpa!"

Billy wraps his arms around N-J and asks, "How's my buddy doing?"

N-J gives Kathy a warm hug and replies, "Great. Let me show you my new baseball glove." N-J races over toward a shelf, removes the glove and darts back. "Look!"

Billy takes a glimpse and asks, "Where did you get this?"

"Papa brought it the other day."

They all take a seat at a table and Kathy says, "Grandma's coming up soon. We're going to celebrate your twenty-first birthday and her seventieth together. Is that okay?"

"At the house?" N-J asks.

"No, your father wants it at the restaurant."

"Okay, I can't wait to see grandma," N-J excitedly replies.

Billy says, "No touching the knives though. You know that, right?"

"I know, grandpa."

"I'm serious now."

Kathy asks, "Do you want anything special for your birthday?"

"Can I go to a baseball game next year and have cotton candy?"

Billy replies, "I think we can manage that. Which team?"

"Grandpa, how could you ask me that?"

Billy laughs while rubbing N-J's hair and says, "Just checking to see if you crossed lines."

"Never, grandpa."

Kathy asks, "Has your sister been visiting you?"

N-J smiles and replies, "She comes every week, mama, and brings me cookies. She knows I love cookies."

Kathy replies, "That's good. I'm glad to hear it. How about your father, has he been around?"

"He came only once this week, when he brought me the glove."

Kathy is now annoyed at Nutsy but doesn't want N-J to know. "He's been busy, N-J. You know daddy loves you."

"I know he does."

While back at The Headquarters after discussing the under bet, Nutsy decides to run a refresher course. So he tapes a large white piece of cardboard on one of the walls.

He writes down with a black magic marker, Bills plus four and Jets minus one. "Alright, not that we're ever gonna see this line on the Jets any time soon, but if someone wants a hundred time teaser with these two teams, what's the line?"

A man relies, "Bills plus ten and Jets plus five."

Nutsy asks, "How'd ya get that?"

"Four plus six is ten. Minus one plus six is plus five."

"What's the wager and what's the vig?" Nutsy asks.

The man replies, "Wager is five hundred and the vig is a hundred if they lose."

Nutsy asks, "Why is the vig a hundred and not fifty?"

"Because it's a teaser bet," the man replies.

Nutsy glances toward Ladro and asks, "What do ya think, Ladro?" In the past, Ladro scrambled the numbers while taking medication for his leg and this has been currently on Nutsy's mind since Ladro already mixed up the slip for Munchie.

"It looks fine to me," Ladro replies.

"Alright, we don't see them as much anymore, but let's do a three-team tease." Nutsy writes on the cardboard, Boys minus three, Pac minus two, and Giants plus four. "Alright, two hundred times. What's the line, Ladro?"

"Really now?"

"Come on. Help the guys out." Nutsy just wants to see if he's right about Ladro not being able to do the calculations any more.

Ladro shakes his head and replies, "Boys plus seven, Pac plus eight, and Giants minus six... no wait, Giants plus fourteen."

"Are ya sure?" Nutsy now knows his suspicions are correct and this slip would probably be screwed up if Ladro was rushing to take the next call.

"Yeah, that's it," Ladro replies.

Nutsy glances toward another worker and asks, "What's the wager?"

The worker replies, "A thousand."

"What do ya think, Ladro?"

"Are you gonna ask me every time you write something down?"

"Maybe." Nutsy looks back toward the worker and asks, "What's the vig if they lose?"

"It would be two hundred."

As Nutsy glances back toward Ladro, Ladro quickly says, "Don't ask."

So Nutsy laughs and continues on with more scenarios.

After finishing his crash course, Nutsy strolls through the park located across the street from the roundabout and takes a seat on a bench. This is a place he comes to every once in a while to gather his thoughts and take in some fresh air.

It's a beautiful park with mature trees, a gazebo, and basketball courts. Concrete paths curve through the park and a large grassy area is in the middle.

On a nice day, residents will picnic on a blanket or just take in some sun while reading books. It's a perfect place to get away from the city but still remain in the city, if that makes any sense.

Most families from this city know very well that this park changes quickly at night. Let's just say, you definitely do not want to get caught in here alone.

While a young boy and his mother stroll passed Nutsy, the young boy notices him and says, "Hi, Mr. Gento. What are you doing here alone?"

Nutsy stands up and gives the lady a kiss on the cheek. He knows them from the neighborhood. Nutsy shakes the young boy's hand and replies, "I come here once in a while to think."

"Think about what?" The young boy curiously asks.

The lady says to her son, "Don't be so nosy all the time." She turns toward Nutsy and says, "I'm sorry."

Nutsy laughs and glances toward the young boy. "Ya really wanna know?"

The young boy nods yes.

"I think about my children when I'm here alone."

"Why about them?" The young boy asks.

"That's enough, it's his private business," the lady says to her son.

Nutsy smiles at the lady and replies, "It's alright." He squats down to glance into the young boy's eyes and says, "One day if you're fortunate to have your own children, you'll remember this day... I think about if I'm a good father to them."

"Well, you're the only one who buys new baseball uniforms for the Little League every year, so you must be," the young boy responds.

Nutsy smiles. He's glad his gesture is appreciated and replies, "I do it because it gives me enjoyment. I like to see the young kids with new uniforms every year."

"What happens to the old ones?"

"We donate them to children that are less privileged than you are."

The young boys replies, "Well, I want to be just like you one day."

Nutsy looks up toward his mother. She knows what Nutsy is mixed up in. So Nutsy replies to the young boy, "Listen to me. Always love your parents and stay out of trouble... and don't forget your studies."

"But I don't like school."

"Learn as much as ya can. One day ya can be anything ya want if ya study enough."

"Like a doctor or lawyer?"

Nutsy rubs the boy on the top of his head and replies, "That's right."

"What if I want to be a baseball player?"

"Then practice hard, but always keep up your studies."

While Nutsy and the lady catch eyes, she kindly gives him a nod thanking him for his comments. She knows Nutsy is trying his best to steer him the right way.

"Okay, Mr. Gento... is N-J okay? I haven't seen him in a while?"

"He's fine. He's staying at a special place now."

The lady doesn't want her son poking any further into this scenario, so she says to him, "Come on. We're late." She says to Nutsy, "Tell Kathy I said hello."

As the lady and young boy stroll away, Nutsy yells out, "Hey son, are you a Yankee fan?"

The young boy turns and replies, "That's my favorite team of all time."

So Nutsy pulls a baseball from his jacket pocket and chucks it toward the kid. "I just got it. It's the new signed team ball."

The kid catches the ball and his eyes open wide. "Wow. Look, ma!"

The lady says, "Nutsy, he can't take this."

"Yes he can." Nutsy glances at the kid and says, "Anytime you look at that ball, you remember what I told you." Nutsy strolls away in the opposite direction.

Nutsy would do anything to deter a young kid from seeking illegal activities. He always wished he never found this path in life, but he had. He doesn't blame anyone or himself for that matter. It's just how his journey in life worked out so far.

He sometimes feels like a hypocrite giving advice like this, but he can't help himself. Down deep inside, underneath his rough looking appearance, is a man with a tremendous heart of gold. Unfortunately, he's not allowed to show it in his line of work and it's the main reason he contributes to multiple charities.

Many people believe it's just a front of his, but it's not. He glances back at this young kid and thinks, that was me back in the day and I had all the choices just like he does right now. I hope he decides on a better path.

CHAPTER 8

Kathy and Billy walk toward their car in the parking lot after leaving the facility. Kathy can't get the thought of what N-J had told her out of her mind. "Nutsy has some nerve. He comes here once for the week? That's bullshit."

As they both slide into the car, Billy hesitantly says, "He's been busy, Kathy, you know that." Billy's not thrilled with it either but can somewhat understand the pressure Nutsy's been under.

Kathy replies, "I can understand if Nutsy's making the right choice, but he's not. There's no excuse for him not to come."

Billy hesitantly replies, "Alright, listen. We both know your husband and he's not gonna change so don't think he will."

As the car now moves down the street, Kathy replies, "I know that, but I'm talking about him visiting his son."

Billy knows exactly where Kathy is heading with this but attempts to play it down. "He brought him a new glove, right."

"Yeah, sure, I don't know what it is with him. He always thinks he can buy his way out of everything."

"You can never downplay a good gesture, Kathy. Let's call it the way it is… on a different note, how much do you have stashed away?"

"I'm not sure, but if I took a guess, maybe a hundred, a hundred and twenty-five."

"That would barely get you through two years."

"Two years? N-J's place alone is over three thousand a month."

"Are you shitting me?"

"No, why do you think I'm so nervous about Nutsy taking a hit on his own?"

"Does Nutsy know how much it costs?"

"Of course, he does. They originally wanted five, but he got them down to three since he knows the manager."

Meanwhile, Squalo sits in front of the glass partition at the jail discussing business with Leo. "I got a young kid I think you'll like. He reminds me of you when you were starting out."

"A Vern kid?"

"No, I think from The Hills."

"You can't trust anyone from The Hills."

"Nah, he's alright. And he already has a beef with Nutsy and his daughter. The best part is, I heard his reputation's on the line right now."

"That's even better. He's got something to prove. How's the girl look?"

"She's cute. She really blossomed up."

"I'm sure. If she's anything like Kathy is, she must be a nice piece of ass."

"I'll tell you one thing. I heard she's tough like Blackie is."

"Blackie still married to that asshole?"

"Yeah."

"Talk about a piece of ass, shit. How's she looking?"

"Listen, I know you'd fuck a gas pipe right now, but let's stay focused, alright?"

Billy pulls up in front of Nutsy's house and slides out of the car with Kathy. As Kathy shuts the car door, she nervously says, "I can't believe this. You really think Squalo wants back in?"

They move toward the front door and Billy replies, "You know me, Kathy. I try to always think two steps ahead. There's a reason why Squalo's making a move right now after all these years."

"Yeah, isn't it because of that fixed bet, or whatever they call it?"

"That could have something to do with it. But there's gotta be more, knowing him."

While Belo and Donnola sit in Squalo's living room, Squalo approaches them with an espresso pot and places it on a coffee table. Belo is curious about something and asks, "Did you know about Leo before we gave Nutsy the proposal?"

"Nah." Squalo is short with his answer since he doesn't want to admit to the truth.

Belo continues on, "I guess it's a coincidence then."

"I guess you can say that," Squalo replies and still keeps it short.

Donnola chimes in and asks Belo, "Why, you have an issue with Leo?"

Belo can't let them know his true feelings. He wasn't too thrilled about going after Nutsy in the first place and now the news about Leo is really concerning to him. "Of course, I don't. I always got along with Leo."

Squalo says, "This changes the whole game for us, fellas."

All Belo can think about at this moment is what his wife had said to him. 'You're siding with the wrong two people. Nutsy's the one you should be with. He's the one that always looked out for you. These two are nothing but assholes.'

Donnola says, "So I opened up with thirty-six on that game. How about you guys?"

As both Squalo and Belo nod in agreement, Squalo says, "I got that punk in The Vern placing bets through some of his friends."

Donnola replies, "Good, this way Munchie doesn't get too overloaded."

Squalo sarcastically replies, "Don't worry, he'll be so flooded, he'll need a rubber raft."

An hour later, Belo drives toward Nutsy's headquarters in The Vern. He pulls over in front of Sista Bar and Grill and waits for a few minutes without getting out of the car. His mind is circling over and over about the decision he made to side with Squalo and Donnola and it's making him sick to his stomach.

Belo finally gets out of his car and enters the Grill. He pauses at the bar and asks the barmaid, "Is Nutsy upstairs?"

She replies, "Hey, Belo, yeah."

Belo nods and heads toward the staircase. He takes a deep breath and slowly climbs the steps while gathering his thoughts. His heart is pounding at this moment. He knows he screwed up royally and wipes the sweat rolling down his forehead.

He bangs on the door and after a minute the door opens and Ladro stands there taken aback to see Belo. Belo hesitantly says, "I need to talk to Nutsy."

Ladro opens the door and replies, "Good luck. He's at the bar."

Belo nervously enters and notices a bunch of people roaming around and catches eyes with Nutsy behind the bar. Nutsy glances back down at the pile of cash he's been counting and doesn't acknowledge Belo at all.

Belo sighs, approaches the bar and asks, "Can I have a word with you in private?"

Nutsy still counts his cash without glancing up and replies, "You and I have nothin' to discuss."

"If you can just hear me out, I –"

"Ya sided with those two fuckin' mutts after how I always treated you? If it wasn't for me, ya woulda never played baseball. Let's not even talk about the charity events I always funded for ya and never took credit for."

Belo glances around. Everyone's eyes are now glued on the two of them. Belo leans toward Nutsy's ear and whispers, "I fucked up, Nutsy. I'm sorry. I wanna make this right."

"I always liked ya, Belo, and considered ya a friend. I don't play second fiddle though. Get the fuck out before I lose my temper."

Belo just stares at Nutsy unsure of how to respond. Nutsy places his cash down and continues on, "Just remember one thing. If I go down because of this, I'll burn all your fuckin' houses to the ground and every other fuckin' thing you own."

Belo knows Nutsy isn't in any mood to listen, so he nods and turns to walk away. As Belo opens the door, Ladro yells out, "I'll walk you downstairs!"

They both step down the staircase and pause by the back of the bar as Belo says, "I tried, Ladro. I feel terrible about this."

"Listen, you know Nutsy. He'll give you the shirt off his back, but if you cross him, he'll write you off. It's just that simple."

"How do I make this right then?"

After all this time, Ladro still can't get Squalo's safe out of his mind. "I heard you're second in line with the code to the safe."

"Yeah, so?" Belo asks.

Ladro deviously glares into Belo's eyes. Belo has a feeling where he's heading with this and asks, "Are you crazy? Do you know how much money is in there?"

"I know exactly. If you really mean what you're saying, prove it then."

"I got my own money in there too."

"You'll get it back plus interest, but we keep the rest to offset the fix if it's really true."

Belo turns away in thought. He's really in a predicament and he knows it. Ladro continues on, "I'll make sure Nutsy knows you did the right thing by us. Your apology means shit right now."

"This is crazy."

"Hey, you know the old saying. Actions speak louder than words… let me know your decision soon." Ladro steps back up the staircase.

Belo asks, "Did you hear about Leo?"

Ladro pauses and turns. "What about him?"

"He's got a good shot to get out because of the new laws."

"That ain't gonna happen. It's only for low-level criminals."

CHAPTER 9

Blackie and Sammy are in Blackie's basement practicing on a few new moves. Blackie loves the idea of working with Sammy. It gives her a partner to sharpen up on her own techniques.

Blackie moves toward the heavy bag and says, "Alright, I'm going to show you a double kick." So Blackie lines up in a fighting stance and thrusts her leg up toward the middle of the bag, pounds it with her foot, pulls back, and then thrusts her leg higher and pounds the bag again with lightning precision.

Sammy watches in amazement and says, "Wow! That was nice, one to the kidney and one to the head."

"Yep, it has to be done quick and hard though. Pop the kidney and break the cheek... have you seen that punk around at all?"

"Every once in a while, he passes me when I'm walking to school."

"Does he notice you?"

"He stops all the time and shoots his mouth off."

"Just keep walking and don't say a word."

"I'm not going to lie, it's not easy. I'd love to pound his face in the blacktop."

Blackie nods. She's knows exactly where Sammy is coming from but has to at least try and keep her out of harm's way. "Just keep walking… alright, let me see your kick."

It's around midnight and Nutsy roams into the kitchen and opens the refrigerator door. The front door closes and Sammy strolls into the kitchen and asks, "What are you still doing up?"

"I'm thirsty."

"It's not good to drink before going to bed."

"The wine dried me out tonight."

Nutsy and Sammy's relationship has been improving lately. Nutsy has decided to lay off her a bit and is hoping she will listen to his advice more often. Up to now, he has been the typical choking father. What are you doing? Where are you going? Who are you going out with?

"Ya know another war might break out soon, right?" Nutsy asks since the thought of Sammy becoming a Navy Seal is still circling through his mind.

"Yeah, I know."

"That doesn't bother ya?" Nutsy asks.

"Not at all," Sammy replies and pecks Nutsy on his cheek. "Go to bed." Sammy walks out of the kitchen.

This has been eating away at Nutsy. He knows she's eighteen and has every right to join the Navy, but the thought of her leaving so young is unsettling to him.

He tries to be understanding but his selfish reasons conflict with his true feelings. How could I let her do this? N-J is not here anymore and now she wants to leave. He knows he's a complex man and has his own beliefs, but this is not sitting right with him.

It's becoming a difficult time in his life. His daughter might be leaving, his son is in a home, and his partners are attempting to squeeze him. What if Billy can really make my dream a reality, he thinks.

He plops on the stool by the island and whips out the same picture he usually gazes at. It's a picture of when N-J and Sammy were kids and tossing a wiffle ball to each other.

Nutsy can't help but smile. He never had this as a kid. His father was a good man but was never home. He worked construction his short life and had a massive heart attack at a young age. His mother was a housewife at the time with no means of support.

This forced Nutsy and his sister to hit the streets at an early age to earn what they could for survival. He's glad that his sister was able to eventually get out from the illegal group she was involved with and go legit, but he still regrets he didn't make the move himself.

Money was easy in the sports booking business in the early days so he figured he couldn't just walk away. It almost became a trap that is haunting him to this very moment.

Kathy strolls in wearing a nightgown and asks, "What are you doing?"

Nutsy slides the photo across the island in her direction and asks, "Remember this picture?"

Kathy picks it up and takes a glimpse. She smiles and replies, "I've been looking for this. Where did you find it?"

"I've had it. I carry it around with me."

Kathy takes another glimpse and says, "I can't believe where the time has gone."

"Yeah, me too. It's moving fast, Kathy."

Up to this point, Kathy has been fighting with Nutsy about taking the deal with his group, but she knows her husband extremely well and that once his mind is made up, there is no turning back.

Although she is not thrilled with it one bit, she has decided to take a different approach with him and seem understanding. I'll give it a shot, she thinks.

While he takes another glimpse at the picture, Nutsy always wanted to ask Kathy a question so he decides to now. "Let me ask ya something. You were always a smart lady and did well in school. Ya probably could've married a doctor, lawyer, or accountant, why me?"

"This is what you want to ask me right now?"

Nutsy nods yes.

"Okay... how about we swap stories? I'll tell you and you tell me," Kathy says.

"Ya know I'm not a story swapper."

"Didn't you always tell me one hand washes the other?"

"So now we're washing hands?"

"My hands are already clean. What about yours?"

So Nutsy and Kathy stare at each other for a moment. Nutsy nods and says, "Okay."

Kathy starts off and says, "Under that tough frame of yours, I always knew you had a good heart. That was important to me in a man."

"There're a lot of professionals with good hearts."

"Maybe so, but they're not you, Nutsy. I know you do because you want to, not because you have to. Most only do because they expect something in return. You were never like that."

"Ya could be in Scarsdale in a nice 10,000 square foot house, with maids, five car garage –"

"You know I didn't grow up that way. I saw my father struggle every day when my mother wasn't around anymore. I was just happy to be able to sit and have dinner with him every night."

"Is that why when the kids were younger, ya always insisted that we all sat at the table and had dinner together?"

"I guess so."

"You're a simple lady, Kathy."

"There's more to life than money, Nutsy. It doesn't always make you happy."

"That's for sure. But it can make life more comfortable."

"Now it's your turn."

"Alright, let me just go to the bathroom first."

"Are you kidding me?"

"I'll be right back." Nutsy stands up and moves away.

Meanwhile, Belinda is thrusting back and forth on top of Munchie in her bed with an annoyed look on her face. She is working too hard and it's throwing off her rhythm.

Munchie's eyes are closed while trying to concentrate but certain things are on his mind and disrupting his performance.

Belinda finally loses her patience and pauses. "I feel like I'm riding a rotten cucumber."

Munchie opens his eyes and replies, "I'm sorry. I was just about there."

"You're a doctor. That thing should be like granite right now." Belinda rolls off of Munchie and gets out of bed. "What's the problem? This has been going on for a few days now."

Munchie stays quiet because he doesn't want to say why.

Belinda continues on, "I want to know. Are you back with your ex?"

"No."

"Are you telling me the truth?"

Munchie hesitantly replies, "I did see her the other day and we had dinner."

Belinda slips on a bathrobe and replies, "Is that so?"

"We had to discuss the kids. That's it. I swear."

"So, why can't your dick get hard anymore then?"

Munchie hesitantly replies, "It has to do with your father."

"What about him?"

"You're better off not knowing."

"While I'm on top of you, you're thinking about my father? Are you kidding me?"

Munchie doesn't reply.

Belinda continues on, "You're gonna tell me what it is. I had enough of this."

Nutsy strolls from the bathroom and plops back down on the stool by the island. Kathy has been waiting patiently for his reply, so she nods at Nutsy. Nutsy laughs and says, "I guess ya didn't forget."

Kathy shakes her head no.

So Nutsy gave his word before and says, "Besides my family, you were the only good person in my life. I always felt different when I was with you."

"What do you mean?"

"It's hard to explain. Ya always brought me into a different world. I know I'm a complex man, but ya made me feel like I had a purpose in life."

"We all have a purpose, Nutsy."

"I know, but there were many times I didn't know if my life was worth anything. All I ever wanted to do was make ya proud. And besides my mother, you're the only other person that ever made me feel that way."

"And you have. You always have."

"Look, I know ya want me to take this deal. But it will eat away at me to lie down to these guys. It's not me, Kathy, I'm sorry."

"Even more than going broke again?"

Nutsy hesitantly replies, "I'm afraid so."

"How did I wind up with the most stubborn guy from this city?"

Nutsy laughs and replies, "It all started in Giovanni's Pizzeria, remember? Ya loved their thin-crust pie."

"Yeah, it was like heaven. They finally reopened after the fire."

"How about we grab a pie this week with an antipasto salad, like the old days?"

"I would love that."

"Okay good, now that's settled, where's the mouse been stashing my money?"

"I donated it to the church."

"Get the fuck outta here."

Meanwhile, Belinda is steaming after Munchie told her the news about her father attempting to use him to push bets onto Nutsy. She can tell this is upsetting Munchie to no end. After all, he can't even perform in bed anymore.

As they sit in Belinda's living room finishing their takeout from The Lounge, Belinda swallows her piece of Chicken Marsala and says, "That's totally insane. You can't get involved like that."

Munchie stuffs a fork full of Penne Alfredo in his mouth and asks, "What do I say then?"

"I know he's my father, but you tell him to fuck off. Do you realize what Nutsy would do if he found that out?"

"How do I tell your father that?"

"Take a Viagra, grow some balls, and tell him. Then maybe we can finally finish one night. I'm getting tired of fucking a ripe banana."

CHAPTER 10

It's about nine in the morning and Belinda is busy sorting through a stack of papers at the body shop when Squalo wanders in.

Belinda peeks up and then glances back down at the papers without acknowledging him. She's still annoyed about the news Munchie had told her.

Squalo notices and sarcastically says, "Good morning to you, too." Squalo takes a seat in front of her desk.

Belinda glances up and stares at Squalo for a moment. "That's the same look your mother gave me when she was pissed off about something," Squalo says.

"How dare you put Munchie in a position like that."

"What position?" Squalo doesn't want to commit to anything just yet.

"You want him to place your bets with Nutsy? Are you losing your mind?"

"It's just for one game. Besides, what do you give a shit for?"

"You're putting him in a bad situation. Do you know what will happen if Nutsy finds out?"

"How would he find out, you?"

"Don't be ridiculous. You know how this city is. News travels quickly around here."

So Squalo just shrugs it off like who cares.

Belinda continues on, "Why? Why do you need to do this? You're the one who made the wrong decision and moved out of this city, not him."

"That's where you're wrong."

"What do you mean?"

"I didn't move out. I was forced out."

"How?"

"Billy made it happen. Nutsy might be innocent, but he's the one who benefited from it all these years."

"I still have no idea what you're talking about."

"It was during the time when your brother was pushing guns around town and I was having issues with your mother. I was a little out of hand at the time and Billy used it against us."

"So, the reason you went to The Plains for greener pastures was all bullshit?"

"Now you're starting to put the puzzle together."

Later that afternoon in The Headquarters, Nutsy wants to make sure everyone is on the same page as far as this apparent fixed game is concerned. "Alright, I wanna rollin' total of all games, especially the Bears / Packers."

"A man asks, "What do you mean by a rolling total?"

"I want you to write down the total of all bets and who they're from."

"That's a lot of work, Nutsy," the man replies.

"What the fuck are ya talkin' about? Ya should know this shit anyway."

"It all goes in the computer program now."

"Then hit the button and print it. I pay for the ink and paper, don't I? I want it hourly. I wanna know exactly who's calling in what and how much."

Belo glances over a newspaper while sitting in his enclosed porch when Bono enters and says, "You wanted to ask me something?"

"This girl from The Vern you know, what's her last name?"

"Gento."

Belo's eyes close while he replies, "Tell me exactly what happened that night."

"It wasn't a big deal, Uncle Belo."

"I'll make that decision."

Bono hesitantly replies, "We were at a bar and some guy started with us."

"You know the guy?"

"He's from The Hills. He's working for some group in The Vern now."

"What group?"

"The Lincoln Lords."

"Go on." Belo knows exactly who this group is since Leo was the one who founded it.

"He started with us."

"And?"

"Sammy flipped him over on the ground."

"Sammy? What did you do?"

"I just watched."

"Stay the hell out of The Vern. And I don't want you seeing her anymore."

"But we're friends."

"I don't care! Stay away!"

"But we didn't do anything wrong."

"Don't test me, Bono."

Nutsy and Ladro pop into Giovanni's Pizzeria which is located right down the street from the roundabout. Giovanni's is a longtime staple of The Vern and is known for their thin-crust pie. It's probably one of the best pizza pies you'll ever taste and has won county awards for it.

They both take a seat at a table and a young waitress approaches and says, "My two favorite guys. The special?"

Nutsy asks, "Why change now after all these years?"

The special is a large antipasto salad for two and two large cheese pies. The Thin-Crust makes it easy to finish a whole pie by yourself, and, after one bite, you'd want to.

While the owner approaches their table and shakes both of their hands, Nutsy says, "It's good to see you're back up and running."

The owner replies, "Thank God I had good insurance. I would've been finished. Presto did the right thing by me."

"I still can't believe that guy went into the insurance business."

The owner hands Nutsy a personal pizza box and says, "Yeah, I know what you mean… it's all there. If the Yanks could ever hit in the playoffs for once, maybe the locals could have a shot one year."

Ladro replies, "That's why you can't bet with your heart. It wrecks you all the time."

"Yeah, you're probably right. I always take a beating on the Giants too," the owner replies.

Nutsy says, "You'd never believe how much action we book on the Giants every week, even knowin' they never cover."

"Don't I know it," the owner replies.

Nutsy replies, "Yeah, they're killin' everyone. Do I need to count this or what?"

"It's all there, five-fifty. One wrong pitch really stuck it up my ass."

Nutsy laughs and replies, "I'm having a party for my son and mother at Sista. I'm gonna need about fifteen pies and antipasto platters."

"Why pizza?"

"How could I not offer the best pizza around town?"

"Okay, no problem… I meant to ask you, what's the deal with this fixed bet coming up this weekend?"

Ladro asks, "What fixed bet?" He's playing dumb.

The owner replies, "I'm sure you heard, the Bears / Packers."

Nutsy asks, "Ya trust rumors? It just cost ya five-fifty on the Yanks."

"You're right, it's probably all bullshit. Good to see you guys." The owner shakes both of their hands and strolls away.

"This fuckin' game's gonna be the death of us, ya know that, right?" Nutsy whispers to Ladro.

Ladro sarcastically replies, "We'll make sure we eat most of the pizza pies and load up on carbs."

"I don't know how ya do it. The world could be collapsing around ya, and ya still don't give a shit."

"It's the guilt, Nutsy. That's what it is. I need some humor in my life."

"What guilt?" Nutsy asks.

The waitress places a large bowl of antipasto salad on the table and asks, "Do you want the homemade wine or house?"

"We'll take the good stuff," Nutsy replies.

The waitress smiles and replies, "I thought so." She moves away to another table.

Nutsy glances toward Ladro and asks, "What are ya guilty about?"

Sammy sits in her living room and dials her cell phone. She impatiently waits for Bono to answer. She already tried calling him a few times, but he hasn't answered yet. He finally answers this time and says, "Hey, Sammy."

"I called you a bunch of times. Is everything okay?"

"Yeah, I'm fine," Bono replies with somewhat of a disappointed voice.

"What's wrong?"

"I don't know. I felt like such a fool the other night."

"Why?"

Bono remains quiet. After explaining to his uncle what had happened, down deep inside he feels embarrassed.

"Why, Bono, tell me," Sammy presses on.

"Because you were the one who did something and I just stood there like an idiot."

"I can show you what I learned if you want?"

"I can't. My uncle doesn't want me in The Vern anymore."

"We can go behind the school. No one will see us."

"You would do that for me?"

"Of course. We're friends, aren't we?"

It's about five o'clock in the evening and Billy and the police captain sit at a table in Joey's Pizzeria in the northern part of town. Billy takes a bite of his Sicilian slice and mumbles, "They still make the best Sicilian."

The officer replies, "They always have and always will. They got it locked up… talk about locked up. Did you hear about Leo?"

"No, what about him?"

"The rumor is, he's got a good shot of getting out."

Billy's eyes open wide and replies, "No way, he's got at least another ten."

The captain replies, "It has to do with this new law these assholes just passed. It's bullshit. It's handcuffing my guys too. They're all pissed off."

"Jesus Christ. You have to be fucking kidding me."

"I wish I was. I thought you and Nutsy should know."

"I thought it was just for soft criminals?"

"If he hits the magic bullets, he's out. That's all there is to it."

"The last thing this city needs is having this degenerate back on the streets."

"I know. It wasn't easy with him years back. Hopefully, he changed."

Billy glances away with an annoyed look.

Meanwhile, Sammy and Bono have decided to meet up in a school parking lot. She is teaching him some karate moves that her aunt had taught her. Bono seems to be a fast learner since he's quick and agile.

Sammy is a powerhouse with natural strength and can easily take Bono down once she grabs a hold of him. Kind of like what she did to Vito in the bar the other night.

It's about an hour later and Sammy and Bono decide to wrap up their session since it's getting dark out. They lean up against a fence to take a drink of water and Sammy says, "You look good, Bono."

"Wow, I can't believe how much you've learned from your aunt. She must be great."

"She's a 3rd degree black belt in two different styles."

"Does she still train?"

"Yup, every night in her basement. You should see the shape she's in at her age. I should only look that good."

"You do, Sammy."

"I what?"

"I don't know what she looks like, but I think you look good."

"You haven't seen her yet."

"Well, I still think you look good."

They catch eyes for a moment and Bono gets a feeling that he has never experienced before.

"Can I ask you a personal question?" Sammy asks.

"Sure."

"When did you realize you were gay?"

"Wow, that's some question." Bono is caught off guard.

"I just always wondered. You could probably have any girl you want."

Bono stays silent and glances away. He feels conflicted at this moment and doesn't know how to respond.

Sammy says, "I'm sorry. You don't have to tell me."

CHAPTER 11

Nutsy and Ladro are driving through town collecting from the week before. They are usually not the ones to collect, but they decided to get some fresh air from The Headquarters and get out for a bit.

Ladro pulls up in front of Mucci, a beer distributor on the west side of town that has been around for many years and supplies Sista with all their beer products.

Nutsy and Ladro step out of the car and enter through the front door. The owner, approximately seventy, is glad to see them both since he finally hit on a week for five-hundred dollars.

Nutsy slips an envelope out from his jacket pocket and places it on the counter. "It's about time. I was gonna write a book about how to never win a bet and make ya the main character," Nutsy sarcastically says.

"You're not kidding," the owner replies.

They exchange a handshake and Nutsy says, "I'm gonna need some backup on Friday. I'm having a party for my son and mother at Sista. I don't wanna run out of anything."

"No problem. You just let me know and I'll have one of my guys bring the kegs right over."

"Don't blow the earnings all in one day," Nutsy says sarcastically.

"Did you open yet for this weekend?" The owner asks.

Ladro whips out a small notebook from his pants pocket and replies, "Yeah, we'll take it now. Who do you like?"

"I'll take the under on the Bears / Packers, two thousand times."

"That's ten G's, you know? Ya never bet that much before," Nutsy says.

"I feel lucky this weekend."

Ladro replies, "A thousand times or higher has gotta be paid up-front. Go get the ten G's."

"Hold on, wait... you think I have that cash laying around? Since when do you collect up-front anyway?"

Nutsy asks, "Then how do ya expect to cover if ya lose?"

"I don't plan on losing."

"Up-front or lower it, it's pretty simple," Ladro replies.

Mucci hesitantly replies, "Alright, nine hundred times for now."

Nutsy gets annoyed and replies, "Yeah, that's convenient, ha?"

"How about we just tell him to fuck off, Nutsy?" Ladro asks while giving Mucci a look.

"It's alright, book the nine hundred times… if ya lose, I'll be here the next day for full payment, ya understand?"

Mucci nods. He can tell they're both annoyed, so he changes the subject. "What time is the party?"

"It's gonna be all afternoon and night. I'm shutting the place down," Nutsy replies.

Nutsy and Ladro drive down the main avenue on the north side of town and Ladro says while sitting in the driver's seat, "Nutsy, we can't give the store away this weekend. This fucking guy never bet nine hundred times in his life."

"Look, I know where ya going with this, but we can't cap the bet. It won't look right. Plus, the up-front payout is already working."

"Yeah, I guess so. At least they can't bet big money without having it."

"Ya said before ya don't believe there's a fix going on. Why ya worried now?"

"What by off chance it's true?"

"We're fucked, that's what."

Ladro drives passed a café on the main avenue and notices Vito popping out of the door. "This kid rubs me the wrong way," Ladro says.

"He's just a low-end punk. Someone will eat 'im up one day."

Ladro decides to pull over and park. "What are ya doing?" Nutsy asks.

"I'll be right back," Ladro replies while he slides out of the car.

Nutsy says, "Don't do anything stupid."

So Ladro approaches Vito standing in front of the café puffing on a cigarette and asks, "What's your deal with Squalo?"

"Fuck off!" Vito replies.

While Ladro laughs at Vito's comment, Vito continues on, "Yeah, keep laughing. You won't be after this weekend once he gets out."

"Who's he?"

Nutsy approaches and cuts in, "What's the issue here?"

Vito replies, "I ain't got an issue. This old man's starting with me."

Squalo and Donnola happen to be driving by and Squalo notices Nutsy and Ladro standing next to Vito. "Pull over!" Squalo yells out.

Donnola pulls over on the side of the street and Squalo quickly slips out of the car then races toward Nutsy and Ladro. "Are they bothering you?" Squalo asks Vito.

"Nah, I don't pay them any mind."

Nutsy replies, "Mind ya own fuckin' business for once, Squalo. You're in the wrong town right now."

"For now."

"For good," Ladro replies.

"Am I talking to you?" Squalo asks Ladro with a stare.

Ladro looks toward the street and notices Donnola sitting in the car. "Ah, there's your butt buddy. I knew he couldn't be too far away."

"That's funny, because you two are up each other's asses more than we are," Squalo replies.

Vito blurts out, "And ya better tell your daughter and that fag she's running around with –"

Nutsy gets up in Vito's face and asks, "What about my daughter?"

"It ain't gonna be like –"

Squalo cuts Vito off and says, "Shut your fucking mouth already. This ain't high school."

So Nutsy presses his forearm against Vito's throat and shoves him backwards against the store window. While Nutsy's eyes glow with fire, he presses his forearm harder against Vito's throat.

The store owner peeks out of the door and catches eyes with Nutsy. The owner closes the door.

Squalo says, "That's enough now."

As Nutsy presses even harder, Vito gasps for air.

"That's it, Nutsy!" Squalo yells out.

So Nutsy finally eases up and says to Squalo, "I'll let YOU know when it's enough."

"All I fucking care about is your decision."

"You'll have it on Saturday."

"I'll be looking forward to it," Squalo replies.

While Nutsy and Ladro race back toward their car, Squalo turns toward Vito and says, "Get in the front seat."

"I have to finish some work for Belinda."

"Fuck her. I said get in the car!"

As Squalo slips in the backseat, Vito slides in the front seat and says, "Is this really –"

Squalo cuts him off, "You listen to me punk. Don't you ever bring his daughter into this again, you got me?"

"What's the difference?" Vito asks.

"The difference is family stays out of business."

"That's his weakness though."

"His weakness is his pride, that's where his decision lies. His daughter will only get your head and kneecaps busted in. You better learn this if you wanna survive these streets."

"Ah, we'll just fuck them both up."

"I feel like I'm talking to a two-year old. It ain't about the brawl, it's about the brains."

"Yeah, well Nutsy looks like a brawl guy to me. How did he last so long?"

"It's only because he hasn't been challenged yet. But he will in no time, trust me. If you wanna be a part of this, you better clean up your fucking act."

"Ya team me up with The Lion if he gets out, and I'll do whatever ya want."

Donnola looks in the rear view mirror and catches eyes with Squalo. They both know they caught a sucker.

"On a different note, what about placing the bets with your friends?" Squalo asks.

"I got two more guys that are willing to do it."

"Alright good, I'll be in touch."

Donnola pulls over on a bridge on top of railroad tracks. Vito opens the car door and slides out. "That was fun." Vito shuts the car door and struts away.

Squalo says, "This kid's never gonna last. We'll give him the shit work for Leo and then toss him."

"Yeah, or until he's in the box, whichever comes first."

CHAPTER 12

Since Billy has heard through a number of sources that Leo has a great chance of getting out because of the new laws New York had recently passed, he decides it's time to gather up The Quad.

The Quad is made up of four big players who invest a tremendous amount of money in The Vern. They control the city development, the political party contributions, and are major influencers within the Municipality departments.

Since they all invest large sums in different projects, it's extremely important to them that The Vern doesn't turn into complete chaos.

Although they all know The Vern is primarily a blue-collar community and has some street crime issues, the last thing they would ever want to see is their money sitting idle, or completely evaporating for that matter.

Billy has known all members extremely well from politics, and in fact, is the person who formed the group years ago. It's been quiet for years and there hasn't been any reason to get everyone together, but Billy feels it's time.

This news about Leo is troubling him for his own personal reasons and he already knows Nutsy's decision, so he calls for a meeting.

The Quad decides to meet at Papo Zetti's apartment. He is known as the "Pope of Fleetville" and started his career as a numbers runner and then went on to owning bowling alleys and then eventually graduated to city property developing.

He currently has four new high-rise towers in the works. The Pope still has a seventies style hair do, wavy and parted down the middle.

His pride and joy is a new tower on the north side that's a block away from the train station. The idea is to make it a high-end tower to attract professionals and higher rents from Manhattan. It's located directly across the street from a park he spent many nights chugging down beer as a teenager.

The second member is a sharp lady named Tiffany Jackson and the sister of Marcus and Staci. They are the children of a prior influential mayor of the city and are all still extremely politically connected. She runs a large hedge fund in Manhattan and is a major investor in the tower projects where she currently has a lot of investor's money at stake.

The third person is Paulie Zetti. He is one of the captains of a large Italian family and is Papo's younger brother. He is quick-witted and fun to be around but can get extremely serious if need be.

Paulie's family, headquartered on the island, has been investing a large amount of money in The Vern. They always considered The Vern to be a pocket of growth and opportunity as long as it remained somewhat controlled.

Last but not least is Gloria Keegan. She is the main shareholder of the largest scrap metal and garbage hauling firm in the county. Everyone always wonders how an Irish woman became the largest garbage hauler.

She married a man named Tommy Gulfo who unfortunately had a massive heart attack at a young age from stress and she inherited the majority of shares. She is just as sharp as he was, maybe even sharper, but definitely more attractive.

She also has been pouring a large amount of money in the city by both buying and investing in new projects. Billy knows they all have a lot at stake here and that is his main angle to get what he wants.

The Pope has an apartment on the top floor of one of the buildings he owns on the north end of town. He converted four apartments into one just for the view since the windows face the south.

The apartment is spectacular with an open floor plan and views of Manhattan. On a clear night, he can enjoy a drink and stare at the iconic Manhattan lights from a large picture frame window.

So now Billy is with the four of them sitting at a large table in the Pope's glitzy dining room. He has an idea of how he would like to present his proposal. It's been a while, so he doesn't really know their current thoughts.

After catching up on family and old city tales, Billy says, "I think we might have a major issue coming up in this city."

Tiffany asks, "Like what?"

Billy replies, "I heard Leonardo has a chance of getting out."

The Pope replies, "That's never gonna happen. He's got many years left."

Gloria asks, "Is it because of these ridiculous laws they just passed?"

As Billy nods yes, Paulie curiously asks, "How do you know?"

Billy replies, "Some of my law enforcement sources say the state's trying to lower costs all around. Depending on the charges and time completed, would determine if you have a shot or not."

Paulie says, "He's right. Some of my own men have a shot too."

So now Billy decides it's time to bring Nutsy into the equation and says, "He's not the only issue we have."

The Pope asks, "What else?"

"Squalo recently backed Nutsy into a corner. He must've known Leo has a shot."

Tiffany asks, "How?"

"He's trying to muscle in on Nutsy's profits. I wouldn't doubt if he wants back in."

Paulie says, "Excuse me ladies, but I hate that no good cock sucking shark. And that other fucking rodent... what's his name again?"

Billy asks, "Are you talking about Donnola?"

"Yeah, he reminds me of that cockroach up in the Senate. I'd take 'em all out if my men weren't being watched."

Billy knows he has their attention and continues, "If Nutsy gets hit big enough because of this, it could give Squalo the reins again in The Vern."

"Nutsy won't allow that to happen to him," The Pope replies.

"I wouldn't be here if I didn't think it could," Billy replies with a serious tone.

Gloria says, "I'm not following you. Right now, it's only speculation. So why is it an issue?"

Billy decides this is his moment and says, "I'm asking if you could back him this weekend if he gets hit hard."

"How much are we talking here?" The Pope asks.

"I'm not sure. I'm guessing anywhere from five to a mill."

"Are you kidding me?" Gloria asks.

"Now you know my concern."

The Pope asks, "It's about this fixed game circulating around town, isn't it?"

Billy nods.

"That's a lot of money," Tiffany says.

"So are the millions you all have in these projects right now. With Nutsy out and Squalo and Leo in, you can kiss it all good-bye. They'll turn this city into a mess, and you all know it."

Paulie says, "Look, I'm not gonna lie, if my family needs to get involved, we're gonna look for a piece of this city, not just investments."

The Pope replies, "That wasn't our deal, Paulie."

"I understand, but I'm just saying. You wanna handle it from the inside, it's your call, and I'll respect that. But you gotta handle it or I will, Papo."

Billy cuts in before the conversation changes paths. "I'm asking you to do this for yourself and my son-in-law. He's always been good to this city. He never got involved with drugs, arms, or that trafficking shit you see all over the fucking news right now. All bets will be off if they control power again."

Billy always made sure Nutsy contributed to political functions and charity events. He always felt it could be something he'd be able to use toward Nutsy's advantage if need be, like right now.

Gloria replies, "I see where you're heading with this, Billy. My husband always adored Nutsy. We do what we can for our families, but this could become dangerous for all of us."

Billy's tone becomes a little louder and replies, "Let me ask you all a question. Do you think Squalo is that much of a moron to not know that WE were the ones that pushed him out of town and got his kid pinched?"

The four of them peek back and forth toward each other.

Billy continues on, "If Nutsy gets crippled and this derelict gets out somehow, good luck filling those towers. You can kiss that money goodbye or maybe even yourselves."

They all stare at each other with concerned looks. Billy has delivered his message successfully like he usually does.

CHAPTER 13

Nutsy and Kathy are having dinner at The Lounge which is located on the west side of the city and close to The Hills section. It's a family owned Italian restaurant that has been around for decades and considered another staple of The Vern.

It could use a little updating from its 70s style decor, but it's known for their generous dishes and homemade cooking. The family has always been major contributors of the city and well respected around town.

Nutsy remembers playing on their little league team when he was younger and cherishes those memories. The owner knew Nutsy was on the team and would give him extra Chicken Milanese when his family came to eat on Saturday nights. Nutsy always loved how they made it and raves about it to this day.

A waitress approaches their table and asks, "Another glass, Nutsy?"

"Sure, why not?"

Kathy asks, "Didn't you have enough already?"

So Nutsy laughs and replies, "How do ya like this? She still thinks she's my mother after all these years."

Kathy replies, "God forbid. That poor lady is a Saint after raising you."

The waitress laughs and asks, "How about you, Kathy?"

Nutsy replies, "Yeah, bring her one too. She needs to lighten up a little for once."

While the waitress and Kathy catch eyes, Kathy nods yes. The waitress moves away toward the next table.

Kathy says, "Lighten up? I think you're the one who needs to lighten up."

Nutsy gazes around and says, "I remember coming here with my parents when I was a kid … it's been a while since my dad passed. He always loved this place and the Clams Oreganata."

"Time is flying, Nutsy."

"I remember that night like it was yesterday… I couldn't believe he collapsed right after I got my zeppoles at the 5th Avenue feast."

"I used to love that feast," Kathy replies.

Nutsy turns his head and replies, "Yeah… me too." He drifts away in thought.

Kathy knows this topic could eventually get Nutsy wound up, so she quickly changes the conversation and says, "I'm taking N-J out for his party and he's gonna stay with us for a few days. I want him to spend time with his grandma."

"Yeah, good idea… knowing her, she'll probably teach him that pinochle game she plays all the time down there."

"What do you think about N-J spending time with her during the summer?"

"Nah, she'll never be able to handle him."

"I guess not… Nutsy, I have to ask you something serious."

"Go ahead."

As the waitress approaches and places a wine glass in front of Kathy and Nutsy, Nutsy sarcastically says to the waitress, "Ya might have to help her walk out, ya know. This is her second glass." Nutsy laughs.

Kathy smacks his arm and replies, "What are you trying to say, I can't handle my drinks?"

The waitress replies, "You should come here when the ladies have their birthday lunches, they seem to handle them just fine." The waitress winks at Kathy.

"Is that so?" Nutsy asks.

The waitress smiles and strolls away.

Nutsy says, "I'll tell ya, you ladies really know how to stick together."

So Kathy now wants to get back to her original question. "All I want is an honest answer. If this game is true, and you aren't with the group, how are you going to cover the losses?"

"I'm gonna ask the mouse in our house for the money."

Kathy stares at him for a moment with an annoyed look. "I'm trying to be serious."

"That's a keeper, ha? The mouse in our house." Nutsy is feeling pretty good right now. While Kathy gives him an annoyed look, Nutsy continues, "I don't know, Kathy. I haven't figured it out yet."

"You're putting the cart before the horse, you know that? That should be figured out before the other decision."

"I'm working on it."

As the waitress approaches and places another wine glass in front of Nutsy and Kathy, the owner approaches and says, "This one's on the house."

The waitress nods and walks away.

Nutsy replies, "Shit, I would've gotten the blue then."

The owner asks Kathy, "He hasn't lost his sense of humor yet, ha?"

While the owner shakes Nutsy's hand and gives Kathy a peck on the cheek, Kathy replies, "Trust me. I still hear these old lines every day."

As the owner and Kathy laugh, Nutsy replies, "Are ya kiddin' me, they're classics."

The owner asks, "Is it true about The Lion?"

"What about him?" Nutsy asks.

"I heard the new laws might let him out."

Kathy's eyes open wide. "On the street?"

"What are ya talkin' about?" Nutsy asks.

"I'm not sure. It's just a rumor I overheard from a customer who gets good information like Billy does."

"This is the first I'm hearin' about this," Nutsy says.

"Billy's gotta know by now, no doubt," the owner replies.

"He didn't say anythin' to me."

"Well, I hope it ain't true. He used to send his guys in here all the time looking for a payout."

"What are they gonna do? Just knock ten years off like that?" Nutsy asks.

"With this being an election year, anything is possible."

Nutsy and Kathy head home after finishing dinner. This news is unsettling to both of them. Kathy is anxious to speak to her father but doesn't want to call him since she would rather discuss it in person.

Nutsy drives north on the main avenue passing Sista and glances out the window. "Wow, busy tonight."

Nutsy continues driving north when he notices a few police cars on the side of the street with their red lights twirling in front of Suzie's Place, a strip joint that has been in the city for decades.

Nutsy says while glancing toward the front of the joint, "Every week there's an issue here now."

"It's not the same, Nutsy."

"Yeah, I heard it's loaded with wannabes. Popping that, ah… what's that shit the young crew drinks now?"

"How do I know?"

"Yeah, I heard it's like, three hundred a bottle or some shit like that."

"Stop by my father's place." Kathy is anxious to talk to Billy. She's more concerned with the news she heard tonight than their current conversation.

"Now?"

"Yeah."

Nutsy and Kathy stand in front of a ranch style house on the north end of town. It's on a quiet street close to an elementary school named Penning. This is the same house Kathy grew up in with her father after her mother had passed away.

Her father was concerned about Kathy being on the south side since he was a single parent and knew he couldn't be home all the time. He eventually made a move north and that's when Kathy enrolled in Penning.

While Kathy presses the doorbell, Nutsy glances around and says, "I remember the first day I stood on these steps."

"Yeah, I couldn't believe it. You had on a guinea T and a hanging cross in your left ear. I was like, is this guy an idiot or what, coming to my house like this?"

Nutsy laughs and replies, "That was the style back in the 80s, remember?"

"Yeah, some style. You and your friends looked like derelicts. No wonder why my father flipped out when you left that night."

"What are ya talkin' about? He loves me."

"Sure, now he does."

"Hey, let's not talk about the three-foot hair doo you had. I couldn't even get through the door that night."

"You could've at least taken the cross out."

"We're still together, right?"

The door swings open and Billy stands by the doorway and asks, "Hey, what's up?"

Kathy replies, "We stopped by to say hello."

While Nutsy and Billy shake hands, Billy asks, "How was The Lounge?"

Kathy replies, "You always get a good meal there."

They all move into the living room and Billy says, "I ran into The Pope earlier, he sends his best."

"Where'd ya see him?" Nutsy asks.

"I bumped into him in Fleetville." Billy doesn't want to commit to the meeting just yet since a final decision hasn't been reached by the members.

"I gotta say, that's some impressive tower he's got going up," Nutsy replies.

Billy asks, "What do I owe this surprise visit to?"

While Nutsy and Kathy catch eyes, Nutsy hesitantly replies, "We overheard some news about Leo. Ya know anything about this?"

Billy hesitates and looks toward Kathy who is anxiously waiting for his reply. "Do you, dad?" Kathy asks.

Billy nods yes. He can't lie to his daughter.

Kathy asks, "Why didn't you say anything?"

"Why stir the pot if the gravy hasn't been put in yet?"

"That's a terrible analogy, dad. How could you not at least mention it?"

"I was waiting to see if there was any truth to it first."

"And?" Kathy asks.

Billy hesitantly replies, "He's got a good shot. That's all I know right now... since it's on the table, I have to discuss something with Nuccio. I'll drive him home."

Kathy sits in the driver's seat of Nutsy's car and presses a button on the dashboard. She mumbles to herself, "How the hell does he drive in this thing?"

She presses a button on her cell phone and waits for Blackie to answer.

Blackie finally answers while drying her hair with a towel in her bedroom, "How was dinner?"

"Fine. You got a minute?"

"Yeah, what's up?"

"You hear anything about Leo?"

"That he's a good poker player right now. That's about it."

"This new law might let him back on the streets."

"What! Are you serious?" Blackie tosses the towel away.

Ladro strolls in the bathroom and pauses to watch Blackie's reaction while she now paces. He can tell something is not right.

Nutsy and Billy sit in Billy's sunroom each with a glass of red wine. They have already started their conversation about Leo, and Billy says, "Nuccio, it was during a time you were rising up and Squalo and his son were making a mess of this city. We had him pushed out."

"Pushed out?"

Billy nods yes and replies, "And we had the kid pinched, too."

"Jesus Christ. What else is hiding up your sleeve?"

"Look, I'm not gonna lie. I was hoping you'd be out of this shit and long gone by the time he even had a shot at getting out."

"Is this what ya meant by, I was voted in?"

Billy nods yes and replies, "You're the one they wanted, not Squalo. I was just trying to do the best for you."

"It's pretty ironic, ha?"

"What is?"

"That this degenerate could get out and Squalo tosses this bullshit my way."

"It's not ironic, Nuccio. A shark knows exactly how to make its moves. I wouldn't doubt if he already knew it." Billy turns away.

Nutsy notices a rare concerned look on Billy's face and says, "I gotta say. I've never seen this look on ya."

"I've been in politics my whole life. I just don't understand what they're thinking about."

"It's all about the fuckin' votes today. Ya know that, Billy."

While Kathy slides out of the car in front of her house, Sammy and Bono head down the walkway toward Bono's car. Although his uncle told him to stay away from The Vern, his feelings have been changing toward Sammy.

Kathy notices them and asks, "Where are you two off to?"

"We're going to the movies tonight."

"In The Hills?"

"Here, at the Park Theater."

"And then what?"

"We don't know yet."

"Keep in touch. And don't forget to stay away from that bar."

Bono says, "Have a good night, Mrs. Gento."

"You too," Kathy replies.

Kathy pauses in her foyer and sighs. This news about Leo is the last thing she would ever want to hear. Her cell phone rings and she answers, "I'm sorry. We got cut off."

Blackie is on the other end pacing in her living room. She has her own concerns about Leo getting out and asks, "Did your father tell you this?"

"Nutsy's talking to him right now."

Nutsy and Billy sit in Billy's car heading down the main avenue. They're taking a cruise around town while finishing their conversation and Nutsy says, "I would've been happy just being second man on the totem pole."

"You wouldn't believe me if I told you."

"Try me."

"I had good information back then, they were ready to make a play at you."

"What play?"

"Do I have to spell it out for you?"

"Are ya trying to tell me they were gonna rub me out?"

Billy nods yes.

"No fuckin' way!"

"Yes way. And the night Ladro's brother got clipped, it was supposed to be him."

"Boy, you're really full of surprises tonight."

Meanwhile, Ladro wanders into the living room and notices Blackie's still on the phone with Kathy and overhears her say, "I guess we'll find out, won't we?"

Kathy replies while sitting at the island in her kitchen, "Let me run. I have a splitting headache right now." Kathy hangs up and tosses the phone on the island.

"We'll find out what?" Ladro is curious about Blackie's conversation.

Blackie hesitantly replies, "The Lion has a chance to get out."

"Impossible."

"Apparently not. And he'll want his money, you know that, right?"

Ladro heats up and replies, "Fuck him! That money cost my brother his life."

"You still think Leo was the gunman?"

"There were only four of us that knew about that job, you, me, my brother, and Leo, unless you were the shooter?"

"Yeah, it was me. What a ridiculous thing to say."

"I don't give a shit, Blackie. He ain't getting a fucking dime from us."

CHAPTER 14

The next morning, Squalo was back at the state jail behind the glass partition having a conversation with Leo. He has been anxious to find out the verdict.

Leo has just told him he is cleared and waiting on the final sign off to be released. Squalo is beaming and can't wait for Leo to get back on the streets.

You would expect a father would want his son to stay clear of any trouble. Not Squalo, he has his own agenda and knows Leo can help him achieve it.

"And the first thing I gotta do is collect my money from Ladro," Leo says.

"I still can't believe you missed him that day. It was a perfect opportunity, a botched job."

Leo peeks toward the guard and stays quiet. Squalo stands up realizing what he had just said. "My mistake. Let me know the day. Hopefully, you'll be around for Nutsy's decision."

"I'll do my best."

Squalo nods and struts away.

Later that day during lunch time, Squalo meets up with Belo and Donnola at the New Row Diner. He couldn't wait to tell them the great news about his son. This brings his agenda up ten notches, Squalo thinks.

While shoving a turkey club into his mouth, Squalo chomps a few times and mumbles, "The Lion did it."

Donnola replies, "No way?"

Squalo nods with a grin. He is ecstatic.

Belo can't believe what he had just heard. This is a whole different game now. It's not just us trying to get some profit from Nutsy anymore if Leo gets out, he thinks.

Belo can't show that he is not thrilled with this news, so he goes along with it and says, "Wow, talk about turning it up a notch."

Donnola replies, "A notch? I'd say a grand slam."

Squalo replies, "Yeah, it's like those cheating pricks last year on the diamond that cost me thousands. Who would've thought they had eyes all over the field?"

All Belo can think about at this moment is what his wife had said to him, but he grins and goes along with it. "Shit, he's gonna need everything. A license, a cell phone, debit card, email."

"You're not shitting. He's gonna be lost for a while," Squalo replies.

Donnola chimes in, "Like a whole new world for him."

After having lunch, Belo hops in his car and heads back toward The Hills. He can't believe the news about Leo and mumbles to himself, "What the fuck am I gonna do now?" All he can think about is what Ladro had said to him about the safe.

He knows Ladro is right and Nutsy would never forgive him unless he did something big to prove it. Words mean nothing right now.

Even then, Nutsy might still never forgive him but at least it's the only way to have a chance, he thinks. Belo whips out his cell phone and holds it for a minute in thought. He finally presses a button and waits for an answer.

Ladro is sitting at the conference table in The Headquarters finishing up a phone call. He looks at his cell phone and says to the other party, "Alright, two hundred times on the Vikings. You're in. Best of luck, I gotta go."

Ladro hangs up the office phone and answers his cell phone, "Yeah, what's up?"

"I get my money back with interest?" Belo asks.

"That's what I said, wasn't it?"

"I can trust you with this?"

"Hey, it's either me or you can lick The Lion's ass when he gets out."

"I can't believe this. Does Nutsy know our deal?"

"This is between you and me right now. I'll let Nutsy know once it's over. He's better off not knowing right now."

"Stop by my office later. I need to look in your eyes."

Later that evening, it's a typical Thursday night macaroni dinner at Nutsy's house. Large glass bowls of Rigatoni and bottles of red wine are scattered across the table with a few meatball and sausage platters.

Nutsy, Kathy, Blackie, Ladro, Sammy, and Billy are sitting around the table. Nutsy peeks over toward Sammy who is glancing at her phone. She's been staring at it all night. Finally, Nutsy has enough and asks, "Ya marrying that phone, or what?"

Sammy looks up and asks, "Are you talking to me?"

"I don't see anyone else starin' at their phone at the table, do you?"

Sammy rolls her eyes and replies, "It just never ends with you."

"And it never will, so get used to it."

Billy cuts in before the conversation gets out of control. He has witnessed this a number of times and asks, "Alright... so what do you have on the menu for the party?"

While Nutsy and Sammy stare at one another, Kathy replies, "We're getting a little bit from everyone."

Blackie asks, "Like what?"

Kathy replies, "Nopp is doing the potato salad."

Ladro says, "I fucking love their potato salad."

Blackie nudges Ladro and says, "Stop cursing at the table."

Kathy continues on, "Zucca is doing the Italian and chicken cutlet wedges. Giovanni's doing the thin-crust pizza."

Billy asks, "Pizza and potato salad? I thought this was an adult party?"

Kathy continues on, "I'm not done yet. Curio is doing the hot dishes, eggplant, Chicken Francese, Penne Alfredo, and sausage and peppers."

Billy replies, "Oh, okay. That's more like it."

"What about the best part, dessert?" Ladro asks.

Nutsy replies, "Turo's doing half and Fleetville the other half... oh yeah, don't forget the Sicilian from Joey's."

Billy asks, "What are you getting all this food for? How many people are coming?"

Kathy replies, "Nutsy invited everyone for this. Probably close to seventy."

Ladro says, "You can count on the stooges showing up."

Blackie asks, "They were invited?"

Nutsy replies, "The invitations were sent out a long time ago."

Ladro replies, "If it's a free meal, they'll be there, especially the weasel."

Kathy says, "Just wonderful."

Billy doesn't like the way the conversation is heading and asks Sammy, "What colleges are you applying to?"

Sammy replies, "I haven't yet."

Kathy glances toward Nutsy hoping he doesn't start with a wise crack. Nutsy stays silent though.

So Billy asks, "How come? Isn't this the time to send in applications?"

Sammy peeks toward Nutsy and hesitantly replies, "I'm applying to be a Navy Seal."

Billy is old school and a patriotic person. "I think that's fantastic."

Nutsy sighs but remains quiet. Billy notices and asks, "What is it, Nuccio?"

"Nothing, it's her bed to make." Nutsy feels the complete opposite but is trying a different approach toward this topic.

"I did some time in the Marines years back. It taught me a lot about life," Billy says.

"I guess I'm taking after you, grandpa."

"I think you'll make a great Seal," Billy replies.

While Nutsy and Kathy catch eyes, the doorbell rings and Sammy says, "I'll get it." She gets up and walks away.

Billy glances toward Nutsy and asks, "I guess you're not thrilled with this, ha?"

"I couldn't even take Kathy out on a date without some of your friends following us. Would you be?"

"Different times, Nuccio. These kids are all over the place today."

"Yeah, that's only because we let them. They need fuckin' ropes today."

Kathy replies with an annoyed look, "How many times do I tell you, no cursing at the table?"

Blackie says, "Between him and his partner, they still think they're in the high school lunchroom."

While Kathy and Blackie laugh it off, Sammy strolls in with Nutsy and Blackie's mother, Carmela. She is an older version of Blackie with jet-black hair, olive skin, and a slim body. She's an exceptionally good-looking lady and speaks with an Italian accent.

"Here she is. My partner in crime," Billy says as he stands up and gives Carmela a hug.

"Where did you find that driver? He's cute," Carmela asks Nutsy.

Nutsy stands up, gives Carmela a hug and replies, "Between you with the guys and Billy with the ladies."

Carmela glances at Billy and asks, "We're not dead yet, are we?"

Billy replies, "Amen to that. How's Florida treating you?"

"You have to come down. It's probably four ladies to one man."

Kathy replies, "He's fine right here, ma. I don't need any of those gold diggers digging their claws into him."

Carmela exchanges hugs and kisses with everyone around the table and leaves Blackie for last. "How's my beautiful daughter doing?"

Nutsy sarcastically replies, "You didn't ask how your handsome son was doing."

"Just look at her. She ages like a fine wine."

"I wouldn't say that, ma. My wrinkles are starting," Blackie replies.

Kathy replies, "Yeah, we should all age like you."

Ladro's cell phone buzzes on the table. Blackie peeks at it and notices Belo's name displaying across the screen. Ladro presses a button to end the call without answering and shoves the phone into his pants pocket.

As Blackie and Ladro catch eyes, Ladro shrugs and says, "Fuck him. He's probably getting nervous."

"Is that right?" Blackie asks as she becomes suspicious.

Carmela asks Sammy, "Where's your brother?"

"He's coming tomorrow."

"I still can't believe he's living there. What a shame."

Kathy replies, "Mom, he's happy and there's always someone around to watch him."

"You two should be watching him." Carmela is old school.

Nutsy cuts in, "Let's not start with this already, alright?"

Carmela replies, "Fine… I'm just saying."

Ladro's cell phone buzzes again in his pants pocket and he slides it out just enough to peek at the screen.

Blackie notices and asks, "Is that him again?"

Ladro stands up and replies, "Let me see what he wants." Ladro moves away from the table and answers the phone, "Make it quick. I'm at Nutsy's house with the family."

Belo is sitting in his parked car at the County Shopping Center parking lot and asks, "I thought you were stopping by my office tonight?"

"I got my nights fucked up. It's Thursday night. You know what that is."

"Yeah, I know. It's macaroni night."

"My coffee's getting cold. So what's the word?"

Belo hesitantly asks, "Do I really have a choice?"

Ladro grins and replies, "I'll be in touch. Don't say a word to anyone. You got me?"

"Yeah, that's exactly what I'm gonna do."

"You have the code?" Ladro asks.

"No, it's in Munchie's office."

"Alright, get it then."

"Sure, just like that?"

"Figure it out. You're a big boy now." Ladro hangs up.

Belo hangs up the call and sighs.

Ladro now approaches the table and takes a seat. Blackie is still wondering why Belo is calling him and asks, "So?"

"So what?"

"Don't answer my question with a question."

So Ladro replies, "He was asking what time the party starts."

Blackie gives him a look like, yeah okay.

"Who gives a shit what he's doing anyway?" Ladro pours another glass of wine and tries to downplay it.

Blackie glares at him skeptically. Ladro notices and asks, "What's the look for?"

"I'm not sure, but I'm sure there's a reason."

Ladro laughs and replies, "You always think everything's something else."

"It always seems to wind up that way, doesn't it?"

Billy asks, "Hey, Carmela, how about tomorrow morning you and I go to Thena's for breakfast?"

"That's a date," Carmela replies.

Nutsy sarcastically says to Billy, "Yeah sure, I see ya every day and I never get asked."

Billy replies, "Carmela always had nicer legs than you did."

They all laugh.

CHAPTER 15

The Quad has decided to have a meeting without Billy to discuss the situation privately. The news is disconcerting to all of them considering the large amount of money that is currently on the line.

The last thing they would want is for bad news to circulate around town. Even more concerning is if bad news reached people from Manhattan looking to rent units in their new deluxe towers.

They are back at The Pope's apartment. He currently has the most to lose considering a majority of his own personal money and livelihood are tied up in the projects.

The Pope starts off the conversation. "I've been thinking hard about this. Do you think Squalo knows we were behind it?"

Paulie replies, "Who cares? We can't look back now."

Tiffany replies, "We did what we had to at that time and Nutsy's been good to this city. I'm not second guessing it."

Gloria replies, "I agree. Before, when Squalo and Leo were at the top, this city was heading downhill quickly. My husband hated those two. Nutsy always treated this city with respect."

Paulie replies, "Look, we all have millions in these projects right now and are looking to attract a better clientele. I don't think we have a choice but to back Nutsy."

The Pope replies, "If Billy's right about this bet, Nutsy can get clobbered though."

Tiffany replies, "It would be peanuts for us compared to the millions we can kiss goodbye. The last thing we want is for these towers to sit empty."

Gloria says, "Besides Billy, Nutsy was the only one out of that group who came to my husband's wake and funeral. My bet stays with Nutsy."

The Pope says, "Alright, let's take a vote. If it's even, we flip a coin, alright?"

They all nod.

Belo wanders into Munchie's office and approaches the secretary at the counter. "Is Munchie in yet?"

"No, he's still at the hospital. Is there anything I can help you with?"

"I left something in his office. Can I go look for it?"

"I'm sorry, Belo, I can't let anyone in his office for privacy reasons. I told you that already."

"I understand. Just tell him I stopped by." Belo walks away.

Belo is now driving north through The Vern and passes Sista Bar on his left. He wonders if he should stop in again but decides he's going to call Ladro instead.

Nutsy sits at the conference table crunching numbers while pressing buttons on a large calculator. The tape on the calculator is spitting out continuously.

Ladro passes by Nutsy and says, "Use the excel, they ain't even selling these tapes anymore."

"Oh, now you're a computer wizard?"

"It's better than becoming a T-Rex, isn't it?"

As Ladro now stands behind the bar, his cell phone rings and he answers, "You get it, or what?"

Belo replies while still driving, "I tried three times already. I don't see it happening."

"We'll do it the old-fashioned way. You're gonna have to help me though."

"No fucking way!"

"Alright, we'll just forget it then. I gotta go."

"Wait. Wait… what will I have to do?"

"I'll stop by later." Ladro hangs up.

Nutsy asks while still crunching numbers on the calculator, "Who was that?"

"Some asshole that wants to set up an account."

"If he's lookin' to set up an account for just the under bet, tell 'im to go fuck himself."

"Yeah, I'll see what he wants first."

Nutsy tears off the tape and sighs. "Shit! Fifty thousand times and rising as we speak."

"And it's only the beginning," Ladro replies.

Nutsy says, "This should be interesting. We got the party Friday night, Saturday we tell the stooges to fuck off, and by the end of the game on Sunday we get our asses handed to us."

"Hey, nothing like going out with a bang," Ladro replies.

"Sure, it's how we said we'd always go down, right? I never thought it could be this soon though."

It's about a half an hour later and Squalo sits in Munchie's office. Squalo stopped in to have Munchie call in to Nutsy, twenty thousand times on the under, and it's making Munchie run back and forth to the bathroom with stomach pains since twenty thousand times equals a hundred thousand in wagers.

After finishing in the bathroom, Munchie nervously enters his office and Squalo says, "Call him now. That was your third shit already. Stop stalling."

Munchie hesitates while thinking about what Belinda had said to him. He really wants to tell Squalo to take a walk and is trying to get up the nerve to.

"Call the fucking guy already!" Squalo impatiently says.

"I can't do it. Go ahead. Tell Belinda anything you want. I don't care." Munchie had enough.

So Squalo gives a smirk and replies, "I knew it. How are those student loans going anyway?" Squalo always has a backup plan.

"What?"

"I'll bet you're still ducking them."

"You know I haven't paid them, so?"

"It would be a shame if news circulated that a well-respected local doctor is purposely fucking the government AND the taxpayers."

"This isn't right, Squalo."

Squalo sarcastically replies, "I can just see it. Local doctor takes out hundreds of thousands in student loans, makes big money, and fucks over the system. That would make a great story. What do YOU think?"

"I can't believe you're doing this." So Munchie nervously picks up the phone and dials while staring at the firm expression on Squalo's face.

Ladro sits on the couch at The Headquarters slurping his coffee while watching the sports reviews on the big screen TV. The office phone rings on the conference table and Ladro yells out to one of the workers, "Grab that!"

The worker picks up the phone and answers, "Sista!"

Munchie nervously replies, "Munchie for Ladro."

"Hold on," replies the worker. He glances toward Ladro and says, "Munchie's on the phone for you."

So Ladro moves toward the conference table and takes a seat. "Go ahead, Munchie." Ladro whips out a small notebook from his shirt pocket and grabs the pen from behind his ear.

Munchie hesitates while noticing Squalo's piercing stare. The longer he hesitates, the more piercing Squalo's stare becomes.

Ladro asks, "You still there, Munchie?"

So Munchie replies, "Yeah, I'm here. Twenty thousand times on the Bears / Packers under."

Ladro laughs and replies, "You'd be wearing fucking diapers that day if you ever bet that much."

"No, I'm serious."

Ladro hops up and replies, "You already called in your bet."

"I feel lucky this weekend."

"Anything over a thousand times has to be paid up-front now."

"Since when?"

"Since Nutsy decided it, that's when."

"Alright, I'll get back to you." Munchie hangs up and says to Squalo, "They want the cash up-front."

"You're bullshitting me."

"Ladro said anything over a thousand times, Nutsy wants it paid up-front."

So Squalo hesitates with an annoyed look. "Alright, I'll be back in an hour. Don't go anywhere."

"Squalo, I have a practice to run."

"I said, I'll be back in an hour," Squalo replies as he stands up and struts away. "I'll fix his ass."

Squalo drives north on the B-R Parkway toward his apartment and presses a button on the dashboard to dial a number through the Bluetooth.

Donnola sits in his messy living room filled with empty beer bottles and newspapers scattered on the floor. The living room furniture is from the 70s and completely outdated.

While his cell phone rings, Donnola swats away the loose papers scattered across the couch and finally answers, "What's up?"

Squalo is still heated about the up-front money and asks, "Would you believe that fucking prick wants the money paid up-front?"

"I don't know who you're talking about."

"Nutsy, you fucking idiot! You never know who I'm talking about. Can't you just read between the lines for once?"

"Squalo, take it easy. I was napping."

"Well, wake the fuck up! How much you got so far on the game?" Squalo leans on the horn and yells out the window, "Let's go you fucking moron."

"I got about ten thousand times and counting. And by the way, you better relax, you're gonna have a stroke," Donnola says.

"Is it me or can nobody fucking drive anymore?" Squalo is all wound up.

"What do you expect? They're handing out licenses like lollipops today. You're gonna lay out the money, right?"

"Not me, the asshole is. And I'll put it back after we hit."

Squalo is now in his apartment and tosses something into the shark tank. "Here's leftover Lasagna."

He moves toward the safe on the wall and cranks the dial back and forth. He swings open the door and removes a pile of cash from the safe. He rolls his finger through the pile and then removes another two piles of cash. "This should be enough."

Billy and Carmela are now having breakfast at Thena's. It's a well-known diner in the northern part of town. "I always loved their pancakes," Carmela says as she takes a fork full.

"I'll take their marble cake any day of the week."

"Yeah, I always liked it myself… Billy, I have to ask you a personal question."

"Yeah, what's up?"

"You and me, we've always been family people. What's this with N-J being at this place?"

"I know what you're saying, Carmela. I'm not thrilled with it either."

"I mean, come on. We'd never do this, would we?"

"I don't know. It's hard to say. N-J's a tough kid to watch sometimes. When he blows, he blows."

"Billy, we all can have our moments at times. He's no different."

"Believe me, I know what you're saying. There's more though."

"I knew it. God forbid my son tells me anything. You will though, right?"

"You're really gonna put me on the spot like this?"

"How long have I known you? If you weren't my son's father-in-law, I might've even dated you years back." Carmela laughs.

Billy nods and replies, "One night, Kathy and Nutsy had guests over. One of the guys was drinking too much and said something derogatory to Kathy when Nutsy walked out of the room."

"What does that have to do with N-J?"

"I'm getting to it. Kathy said something to him and the guy made a real nasty gesture toward her. N-J happened to see it and grabbed a knife from the cheese platter and charged at him."

"Oh, my God, what happened?"

"Blackie saw N-J grab it and tackled him to the ground. Luckily, N-J just nicked the guy's arm."

"Then what happened?"

"When Nutsy walked back into the room and heard what happened, apparently it wasn't a pretty sight."

"No wonder Nutsy hasn't said anything."

"After months of discussions, we all decided N-J needed to be watched and in a calm environment."

"Too bad he didn't take after your side of the family. He's cursed with his father's temper."

"So far he seems alright there, so we're all happy about that."

CHAPTER 16

Squalo returns to Munchie's office with a large brown paper bag and says to him, "Here's a hundred and fifty thousand cash. Call in thirty thousand times."

"This is insane, Squalo. Why are you putting me in a position like this?"

"Because whether you like it or not, you're a part of us. Especially, since you're still fucking my daughter."

"It's not like how you make it sound."

"Really now? You take her out for dinner? To the movies? For a walk down the street holding hands? No, you take her to your apartment so you can have your way with her. That's what you do."

"She's the one who wants to keep it quiet."

Squalo laughs and replies, "I gotta say, you're a doctor but ain't too sharp when it comes to the ladies. And you better not fucking lose it." Squalo struts away.

Ladro and Blackie both stopped home for lunch and just finished a quickie in their bedroom. While Blackie buttons her pants, she says, "We have no choice but to cut him in."

"I told you already. I ain't giving that dickhead a dime." Ladro slips on a sweater.

"That's a mistake. It was all over the news that over a hundred grand in cash went missing." Blackie sits on the edge of the bed and slips on a shoe.

"Yeah, like you can trust those news people. They talk shit all the time. As far as I know, the gunman took the fucking money."

"You know what you're doing, right?"

"What?"

"You're convincing yourself of a lie."

"Call it what you want. That money cost my brother his life. That's what I know."

"Leo isn't going to give a shit –"

Ladro yanks down his pants and points to a large nasty gash on the side of his leg. "You see this, ha? Every day it reminds me of watching my brother take bullets in his back like fucking cattle getting slaughtered."

Blackie remains quiet. She knows this is a sensitive issue with Ladro and will set him off. She's concerned about money that is owed to Leo from a robbery back when she was still somewhat involved with the group.

This was a job she regrets to this day. Leo knew about Ladro's skills at the time and asked her to bring him in on it. It appears that Leo had his own agenda that day but it was never proven.

Ladro continues, "And God help him if I ever find out he pulled the trigger."

Nutsy decides to take a quick drive over to the sports complex. He now gazes at it by the same rusty fence he usually stands by. This time he brought a large drawing pad to sketch on.

While he sketches, he intently gazes back and forth at the field and pad deep in thought. He flips over to the next page and continues sketching.

He pauses for a moment then tears off the page, crumples it, and tosses it into a rusty garbage can close by.

He flips to the next page and starts sketching again. His cell phone rings and he slides it out from his pants pocket and answers, "Yeah, what's up?"

Ladro is on the other end at The Headquarters now. "Where are you?"

"I stopped by the sports field for a minute."

"Well, you might wanna get here. The under bets are starting to fly in."

"Give me a few minutes." Nutsy hangs up and continues sketching since he doesn't want to forget his current ideas.

Billy and Carmela walk into N-J's facility and pause by a desk in the lobby. The perky lady who usually greets the visitors notices Carmela and says, "Mrs. Gento, wow, what a surprise."

"Someone had to bring the sun back up here."

"You surely did, today is a beautiful day. Kathy already signed him out for the weekend. You can take him now if you want."

Billy replies, "That was our plan."

"He's in the back room."

Billy and Carmela enter the back room and Carmela asks, "Where's my boy?"

N-J sits on a chair with his back toward them watching TV and quickly turns. "Grandma!" N-J bolts toward her and wraps his arms around her. "It's our birthday."

"I know, our special time together."

Billy says, "Grab whatever you want to take home for the weekend."

N-J races toward the shelf on the side wall and says, "I only care about my glove." He grabs it off of the shelf and darts back to them.

Carmela says, "Wow, you're fast, you know that?"

N-J nods his head yes in agreement.

"Are you ready?" Billy asks.

N-J nods again and says, "I can't wait."

"Alright, let's go then," Billy replies.

Carmela asks, "What about clothes?"

"I still have some in my room."

Blackie has just finished up a meeting with a customer in her office. As she turns to move behind her desk, Blackie recognizes Belinda's voice in the background. "Do you have a minute to talk?"

So Blackie hesitantly turns already knowing who it is and says, "This is where I work, just so you know." That was a polite way of telling Belinda to keep it calm.

"I'm not here for any trouble." Belinda walks into her office. All Belinda can think about is how nice it must be to work in an environment like this. "Can I sit?" Belinda asks.

Blackie nods yes and they both take a seat. "Is it safe to assume you're not here to set up a checking account?"

"I came here to talk to you personally."

"About what?"

"You heard about my brother, right?"

Blackie nods yes with an annoyed look.

"Trust me, I know exactly how you feel."

"So, you made a special trip here just to tell me that?"

Belinda shakes her head no.

"What then?"

Belinda hesitantly asks, "How did you get out? How did you make the move?"

"From the group?" Blackie asks with a confused look.

Belinda nods yes.

"It was Nutsy's doing. He pressured me to get out."

"You're lucky. My brother would never do that for me."

"I fought him hard in the beginning, but now I'm glad I did it."

Belinda hesitantly says, "I always envied you in a good way, if that makes any sense."

"It never seemed that way to me."

"I have. You're a good-looking lady who eventually put it all together. Look at me? I'm middle-aged and still wrapped up with this bullshit."

"You seem to be doing alright."

"You know I've been seeing Munchie, right?"

"Get the hell out of here?" Blackie replies with a surprised look.

"Yeah, we've been keeping it quiet though... but I know he'll never take me seriously with what I'm involved with."

"He already knows, so what?"

"It's me. I can't help it. I feel like a piece of shit when I'm with him."

"Why are you telling me this?"

"I'm asking you for your help to get out."

"What about the bullshit with my niece?"

"Why do you think I haven't given out the word yet?"

Blackie just stares.

After finishing his sketches at the sports park, Nutsy strolls into The Headquarters and takes a seat next to Ladro at the conference table.

Ladro hangs up the phone from taking a wager and Nutsy asks, "What's the damage so far?"

Ladro replies, "About four hundred right now."

Munchie nervously drags in with a worker from the bar downstairs and approaches the conference table. The worker says, "He wanted to come up. He has cash for a bet."

Nutsy nods to the worker and the worker exits the room. Nutsy notices a concerned look on Munchie's face and asks, "What do ya got?"

Munchie dumps the pile of cash on the conference table and replies, "Thirty thousand times on the under."

Nutsy leaps up and yells, "Are ya fuckin' kiddin' me?!"

Munchie doesn't respond. He's extremely nervous and it shows on his face.

Nutsy asks with an annoyed look, "Now you're tryin' to take advantage of us, ha?"

"No, not at all. I just feel lucky," Munchie nervously replies.

So Nutsy stares into Munchie's eyes for a second but Munchie quickly turns away. He can't maintain eye contact. Nutsy gets a strange feeling inside that there's more to this than it seems.

Ladro also gets an odd feeling and says to Nutsy, "I'll toss him down the steps if you want me to." Ladro wants to see Munchie's reaction.

While Nutsy maintains his intense gaze toward Munchie, Munchie nervously looks up and down. He can't keep eye contact.

"What is it? Ya can't even look me in my fuckin' eyes right now," Nutsy says with a stern voice.

Munchie feels horrible about this and turns away. He was never a good poker player either.

Nutsy can read Munchie like a book and moves toward the bar. "Have a scotch with me. We gotta discuss a few things."

"I need to get back to the office."

"Not right now ya don't."

Since Nutsy decided to close Sista after lunchtime, Kathy left work early to decorate the bar and set up for the party. She wants to make sure the place appears special for her son and mother-in-law. After all, turning twenty-one and seventy are both milestones.

While taping a "Happy Birthday" sign on the wall, Kathy notices Munchie coming down the staircase from The Headquarters breathing heavily and asks, "Is everything okay, Munchie?"

Munchie gives her a kiss on the cheek and says, "I guess you can say that."

"You'll be here later, right?"

"Of course, I will. I have to run, see you in a few hours." Munchie races out since he doesn't want to carry on with this conversation any further.

Kathy thinks his behavior is odd but continues with the decorations since time is of the essence.

Nutsy paces back and forth in The Headquarters while steaming after his conversation with Munchie. "If I didn't know this potato chip eatin' fuck since he was a kid, he'd be licking balls in Times Square right now."

"I say we hit Squalo's safe now and call a spade a spade."

As Nutsy and Ladro stare for a moment, Ladro can sense that Nutsy is toying with the idea so he continues, "Why wait to see if we need it? They're trying to bury us now."

"Do it!" Nutsy replies without any hesitation.

So Ladro whips out his cell phone and dials. He's finally getting closer to his goal.

CHAPTER 17

Belo is now sitting with Squalo and Donnola at the same diner in New Row that they usually meet at to discuss business.

Belo's cell phone rings and when he sees Ladro's name on the display, he quickly answers it. He doesn't want Squalo or Donnola to notice who's calling. "Yeah," Belo says as he moves away from the table.

"It's off," Ladro replies.

"What are you talking about?"

"How many fucking ways could, it's off mean?"

"I mean, why?"

"It's too risky. Plus, they'll know who it was."

"What about –"

Ladro hangs up. He has no interest in continuing with this conversation.

Nutsy glances toward Ladro and asks, "And what's this bullshit about ya making side deals now?"

"I was just trying to get us the code, that's all."

Nutsy stares at Ladro for a moment then asks, "Am I gonna have to start worrying about you too?"

"If wanting to cover our bets is something you have to worry about, then I guess so."

Belo stands by the entrance of the diner for a minute before heading back to the table. He had every intention of trying to make things right with Nutsy, now it all changed again.

Belo approaches the table with a disappointed look and Squalo asks, "Is everything alright? You look like you saw Casper."

"I'm fine," Belo replies and takes a seat.

As Vito now approaches their table, Squalo glances at his watch and says, "I guess you can't tell time."

"I couldn't find this place. I'm not from this city," Vito replies.

"Don't you have maps or whatever that shit is on your phone? Take a seat," Squalo says.

While Vito nods toward the other two to say hello and takes a seat, Squalo asks, "Is your friend good with the bets?"

"No, he said he needs the cash up-front."

Squalo glances toward the guys and says, "This is bullshit. What bookie does that?"

Donnola chimes in, "A bookie that's running scared, that's who."

Vito asks, "What do ya want me to do?"

"I'll get back to you," Squalo replies.

Nutsy strolls into Munchie's office and pauses by the secretary sitting at a desk. The secretary glances up after hanging up from a phone call and says, "Hey, Nutsy, go to the second room."

Nutsy strolls into the second room and then takes a seat on the examining table. About a minute later, Munchie nervously enters and says, "Nutsy, I –"

"This is how I decided it's gonna play out. We're gonna hold the cash and if the over hits, we're keeping it. If the under hits, we're giving ya back the cash and you're telling Squalo we said it never got booked."

"Nutsy, –"

"I'm not finished. And that includes your wagers too. You understand?"

Munchie knows he screwed up royally with his decision and remains silent with a disappointed look.

Nutsy continues, "Alright good… on a different note, I've been having a lot of gas lately. Kathy told me I'm stinking up the house."

"Lay off the red wine for a while."

"Do ya think it could be the chicken and broccoli from Tyfoon's?"

"What the hell are you eating that for? You're Italian, aren't you?"

"Ah… I still like it. What can I say?"

"You heard they might be going out of business, right?"

"Those places don't go out, they somehow burn to the ground first."

"Yeah, somehow. Do yourself a favor, stay away. God only knows what's in that chicken."

After visiting Munchie, Nutsy strolls back into Sista and glances around. The place looks spectacular with the way Kathy decided to arrange the decorations.

Nutsy says to Kathy who is now putting the final touches on the bar, "I told ya to be a decorator, didn't I?"

Kathy replies, "You know I always loved this."

"I'll be right down," Nutsy replies as he steps up the staircase.

Nutsy enters The Headquarters and Ladro gives him a nod by the bar. Nutsy approaches Ladro and whispers, "Hit it tonight. It's time to bury these cocksuckers."

"What time?"

"As soon as the stooges all arrive say hello and slip out."

"How do you know they're coming?"

"Are ya kidding, any chance that prick gets to bust balls, he will."

Ladro grins, his goal is near.

Sammy and Bono are in the back of a schoolyard practicing their karate. Sammy thinks Bono is gaining confidence and his technique is improving since he's agile and a fast learner.

Sammy is blessed with raw strength and her moves are becoming precise with explosive power.

Although it's a cool fall afternoon, sweat still rolls down both of their foreheads. "Let's take a break," Sammy says. So, they both lean against a fence to take a rest.

While smiling toward each other, Bono leans in and pecks Sammy on the lips. Realizing what he had done, he quickly pulls back and says, "I'm sorry."

Sammy is shocked and now totally confused by his actions. She remains speechless since she doesn't know how to respond.

Bono glances away after trying to figure out what he had done. It was an impulse he had never felt before and feels totally awkward and confused.

So now Sammy asks, "What was that for?"

"I don't know, Sammy. It just happened. I'm sorry."

"Don't be sorry." Sammy and Bono catch eyes and Bono leans back over and gives Sammy another kiss. This time it seems more intimate.

It's about four-thirty in the afternoon when Nutsy and Kathy decide to go home to freshen up for the party. The food is being delivered at five-thirty at Sista so Nutsy is rushing around. He passes N-J in the kitchen and asks, "So who do ya like this weekend?"

"I like the Packers."

Kathy passes by and says, "Leave him out of this stuff."

"The funny thing is, for some reason, he's usually right," Nutsy replies.

"I still study the numbers every week, Papa."

Kathy shakes her head. She knows N-J can't gamble where he is but still doesn't like the idea of him even thinking about it.

"Do ya think the Bears' game is gonna be high scoring or low?" Nutsy asks.

"Nutsy, come on now!" Kathy says with an annoyed look.

"Papa, how could you ask me that? High scoring, Rodgers is like a machine."

"I hope you're right, N-J."

"I'll be right, you'll see."

"Don't you have to go back and set up the food?" Kathy wants this conversation to end.

Sammy wanders in glowing after her afternoon with Bono. "Where were you? I've been waiting to see you," N-J asks while giving Sammy a hug.

"I had to help a friend out with something."

Nutsy asks, "What friend, that army kid?"

Kathy replies, "His name isn't army kid. It's Bono."

"You're still friends with him?" Nutsy asks.

Sammy's smile beams across her face as she nods yes. Kathy notices and says, "You look happy today."

"Are you in love, Sammy?" N-J asks since he's extremely perceptive and notices the sparkle in Sammy's eyes.

"No silly. I'm not in love."

"Ya better not be," Nutsy replies as he moves away. "I'm going. I'll see everyone later." Nutsy walks out.

Sammy takes a seat at the island. Kathy can tell she has a glow about her. "Did anything happen today?" Kathy curiously asks.

"Nothing, ma," Sammy replies. She doesn't want to admit to anything yet.

Blackie and Ladro are in their bathroom getting ready for the party. Blackie has on a gorgeous short black dress which shows off her tan, toned legs.

Ladro has also decided to dress in all black. Blackie slides lipstick across her lips and says, "You haven't worn that in years."

"You keep things long enough and they come back in style, right?" Ladro laughs and strolls away.

Blackie watches him walk out of the bathroom and says, "You look like you're doing a job tonight."

"I could only wish that was the case. I'm just glad I still fit in this thing."

Belo is now in his bedroom pulling up his pants while Linda walks in and asks, "Is your issue with Nutsy straightened out yet?"

"No."

"Why not?"

"I tried but he blew me off."

"This is just great. How am I supposed to look him in the eyes tonight?"

"How do you think I feel going to this thing?"

"You're the asshole who screwed up, not me." Linda races out of the bedroom and yells out, "How did I get stuck marrying a moron?"

Belo sighs. He knows he's in a tight spot.

Linda steps down the staircase and says, "They talk about blondes. It's all the good-looking guys that are idiots."

Squalo sits in the back of a café on the main avenue he visits frequently in The Plains. While he slurps his espresso with his pinky in the air, Donnola roams in and takes a seat. "You want one?" Squalo asks.

"Nah, I don't drink that shit anymore. It screws up my stomach."

"You're Italian, aren't you?"

"What can I say? It gives me the runs."

A waitress approaches them and asks, "Do you want anything, sir."

Squalo sarcastically says, "Yeah, get him a cup of milk with a nipple on it."

The waitress attempts to hold back a smile. Donnola replies, "I'll take an unsweetened iced tea." The waitress nods and moves away.

Squalo says, "Unsweetened iced tea? The whole world's going nuts with all this garbage. Grilled chicken salads, green tea, and what's that other green shit you eat now?"

"Are you talking about kale?"

"Yeah, I think that's it."

"It's about eating healthy today."

"Who gives a shit? We're all croaking one day anyway."

"The idea is to last as long as you can, isn't it?"

"For what, take a thousand pills and run back and forth to the doctor? Not me, I'm gonna enjoy until I drop one day."

"Who cares about this? Are all our bets in yet?"

"Most, as far as I know. We're gonna see Munchie later anyway."

"What time are you picking Leo up tomorrow?"

"In the morning. I can't wait until I see everyone's expression tonight when I tell them."

"Why say anything?"

"You really think I give a shit about the kid's or that hag's birthday?"

"Look, the mother is one thing, but the kid?"

"Ah, fuck him too. Maybe I'll give him a knife tonight and let him have some fun."

"What's wrong with you lately?"

"Since when do you care?"

"Let's just change the subject, alright?"

Kathy is now in her bedroom placing clothes in a drawer from a basket of clean laundry. She has asked Nutsy a thousand times to put his clothes away, but he hasn't yet. While she rearranges a drawer full of socks and underwear, she pauses when she feels something odd under them.

She slides out a pad and takes a glimpse. It's the same pad Nutsy was sketching on at the sports park. She curiously flips to the next page and stares at it for a moment.

While she flips to the following page and stares, a tear rolls down her cheek. The more pages she flips through, the faster her tears flow.

"Kathy, where's the toilet paper? There's no more!" Carmela yells from the hall bathroom.

Kathy quickly slides the pad back under the clothes in the drawer and wipes her tears away. "I'm coming."

Sammy slips on a sleek black dress and glances at a mirror over her bedroom dresser. She plays with the top strap covering her shoulders since she wants it to look perfect.

She always admires how her aunt looks in black, so Sammy's trying to following in her footsteps. The black dress is a little higher than her knees showing off her firm calves and the bottom of her thighs.

She dials a number on her cell phone and waits for an answer. Bono finally answers and says, "I'm sorry about before. I don't know what got into me."

"You don't have to apologize for your feelings."

"That's just it. I don't understand what I did."

"You're stopping by later, right?"

"I'm not sure if it's a good idea. I think my uncle is going."

"So, what's the difference?"

"I'll see, Sammy. I can't promise though."

"Just try. I have to go." Sammy hangs up.

Ladro opens a closet in his kitchen and pulls out a large bottle of pain relievers. He dumps a few onto his palm and pauses. "Fuck it." He dumps a few more onto his palm, then chucks them back into his mouth.

He places the bottle back onto a shelf and opens the refrigerator then chugs from a gallon of milk. He takes another swig just to make sure all the pills washed down completely.

Blackie looks stunning as she walks into the kitchen. Her hair is teased back on the sides and a little fluffy on top. Not exactly, but close to an 80s style hairdo.

She glances toward Ladro and says, "I can't believe we're both wearing all black tonight. You should change."

"Not me, maybe you should."

"Who's the one who wears black all the time?"

Ladro laughs and asks, "Does it really matter?"

"People are gonna think we're doing a job."

"Sure, maybe fifteen years ago." Ladro slips out a long slim knife from a drawer and slides it into his coat pocket.

Blackie notices and asks, "What are you taking that for?"

"Just in case any of the stooges screw around. I'm not taking my piece." The last thing Ladro would want, is getting busted hitting the safe with a pistol on him.

"Look, I don't want tonight being all about them. I want us to enjoy ourselves."

"Oh, don't worry. I plan to."

CHAPTER 18

Nutsy is now helping some of the workers set up food trays and a liquor table at Sista. His plan is to have a buffet style dinner and a liquor section so everyone can help themselves and mingle around.

The place looks spectacular because of Kathy's decorations and it's all starting to come together. Nutsy stands in the middle of the room and whispers, "Wow, this place looks great."

So he glances toward the workers and says, "Alright, go home and get freshened up. I want ya all to enjoy yourselves tonight."

While they all nod and begin to walk away, the barmaid turns back and asks, "Nutsy, would you mind if I brought my friend tonight?"

"Of course not, who's the lucky guy?"

"A guy from town I started dating recently."

"I know 'im?"

"No, I don't think so. He's younger than me."

"Ah, robbing the cradle, ha?"

"I guess so. Thanks," the barmaid replies as she heads out.

Billy stands in a nice tailored suit at Nutsy's front door and presses the doorbell. The door finally opens, and Sammy stands there with a glowing smile and says, "Look how handsome my grandpa looks."

"Never mind me. You look beautiful, Sammy. You should wear dresses more often."

"You know dresses aren't my thing, grandpa."

"I know," Billy replies as he enters the foyer.

N-J roams into the foyer with a new tailored suit on and says, "Hey, grandpa, we almost look the same."

"It looks better on you than me."

"You're just saying that."

"Are you kidding? Look how handsome you look."

N-J smiles and Sammy says, "That's the truth, N-J, you do."

Meanwhile, Squalo leans on Donnola's doorbell impatiently waiting for him to answer. "What the fuck is this chipmunk doing?"

Squalo bangs on the door a few times. The door finally opens and Squalo asks, "What are you pulling it or something? Let's go."

"Come in for a minute. I have one more thing to do."

Squalo enters the apartment and sees crumpled up wrappers and empty beer cans scattered across the couch and floor. "How do you live like this? I feel like I'm in a dorm room."

"I was gonna clean today, but a few things got in the way."

"Bullshit. You should be ashamed of yourself. I'm afraid to even sit in here."

"Ah, come on. It ain't that bad."

"Go do what you have to do. I wanna get the fuck out of here before a rat bites my ass."

Billy, Sammy, and N-J sit at the kitchen table waiting for Kathy and Carmela to finish getting ready. Billy glances toward N-J and says, "Remember, no touching the knives tonight."

"I know, grandpa."

Kathy and Carmela walk in and Kathy reconfirms what Billy said, "He's serious, N-J. I don't want any issues tonight."

Carmela says, "He'll be fine. Stop worrying."

Kathy dials her cell phone and waits for Nutsy to pick up.

Nutsy stands by the bar at Sista and answers, "Yeah."

"How's it looking so far?"

"Everything looks great. I think you'll be happy."

"I meant to ask you. Did you give the guys your decision yet?"

"No."

"Why not?"

"Tomorrow night, I am."

"I don't want any of this crap interfering with this party if they show up."

"I haven't even been thinkin' about it."

"You should've told them already. This is a mistake."

"Like ya not tellin' me about my sister training Sammy?"

"I knew you knew already."

"Is that right?"

"That's right. We'll see you in a half hour." Kathy hangs up since she doesn't like the way the conversation is heading.

Ladro is in his garage fumbling through a cardboard box. He pulls out a drill and places it onto the cement floor. He fumbles again and pulls out a small metal box. He flips open the lid and slides out a thin drill bit.

"Ladro! Where are you?!" Blackie yells from inside the house.

Ladro nervously opens the trunk of his car and places the drill and bit inside and slams the door shut. "I'm coming!"

Ladro wanders into the kitchen and Blackie asks, "What are you doing in the garage?"

"I thought I left something in my car."

"Like what?"

"My ear buds."

"Since when do you give a crap about wearing ear buds?"

"I don't. I figured I'd give them to one of the kids."

She is not a fool and asks, "Is there anything going on tonight that I should know about?"

Ladro laughs. "Come on. Let's go. You're getting paranoid in your old age... by the way, you look stunning tonight."

"Yeah sure, change the subject."

Ladro peeks at his watch and with a gleam in his eyes says, "You know, we still have about fifteen minutes."

CHAPTER 19

Nutsy greets a few of the local store merchants at Sista that are still bringing in food trays. With just a few more finishing touches, the party is ready to begin.

Blackie and Ladro are the first to show up since Blackie didn't take Ladro up on his fifteen minute proposal. Blackie glances around and says, "Wow, you did good here, Nutsy."

Nutsy replies, "Nah, this was all Kathy's doing. She spent the day here decorating."

Blackie says, "She always had the magic touch. I'll be right back. I have to use the ladies room."

While Blackie moves toward the bathroom, Ladro approaches Nutsy and whispers, "I'm all set."

"No drinkin' until it's over."

"I'm not a rookie, you know."

"It ain't like you've been in trainin' either."

"Shit... I've been doing a hundred push-ups every night."

A few guests wander in and exchange kisses and handshakes with Nutsy and Ladro.

Kathy walks in with Sammy, N-J, Billy, and Carmela.

N-J is hypnotized by the décor. His eyes scan the room while he takes it all in.

It's about a half an hour later and the room is filled with guests mingling, drinking, and eating. Low music softly plays in the background. Of course, Nutsy has on his classic rock playlist.

Squalo and Donnola roam in and approach Belo and Linda standing by a corner of the room.

Ladro takes a glimpse toward them and whispers to Nutsy, "The stooges are all here now."

"Yeah, anything for free," Nutsy sarcastically replies.

So now the three of them decide to say hello and approach Nutsy and Ladro standing by the bar. Squalo starts off with his usual, "Gentlemen."

They all exchange handshakes and Nutsy replies, "Food and drinks are on the side. Help yourselves."

Belo replies, "The place looks great, Nutsy."

As Nutsy just gives a nod, Squalo decides this is a great time to break balls and bring up his son. "I'm not sure if you heard the great news, but Leo made parole."

Nutsy responds, "Good for him." Nutsy catches eyes with Belo who doesn't appear too thrilled with the news.

Munchie and Belinda roam in and pause by the men at the bar to say hello. They all exchange kisses and hugs. Squalo glances toward Belinda who is dressed in a gown and says,

"Look at my beautiful daughter all dressed up for once and out on the town."

Belinda's eyes roll as she turns away. She knows her father is just breaking her horns.

So Nutsy catches eyes with Munchie who appears a little edgy and says to Belinda, "Ya must be excited to see your brother again soon." Nutsy knows Belinda hates him.

"It's only if he makes parole, which is still a long shot."

"Oh, I guess your father hasn't told ya yet," Nutsy replies to stir the pot.

"It's true?" Belinda asks Squalo.

So Squalo gives Nutsy a stare since he wanted to be the one to let Belinda know. It never looks good hearing news second hand. "Yeah," Squalo replies with an annoyed look.

"How come you didn't tell me?" Belinda asks.

"I was going to," Squalo replies while still glaring at Nutsy.

Nutsy takes this opportunity to stir the pot even further and says to Belinda, "Hey, just look at it this way, ya have a partner to help out now."

Squalo replies, "Thanks for NOT minding your own business." Squalo rudely struts away with an annoyed look.

Meanwhile, Billy is on the other side of the bar engaged in a conversation with Gloria, one of the main players of The Quad. They have always enjoyed each other's company.

Tonight, is starting out no different. "You look fantastic, Gloria, I have to say."

"You know, I'm still waiting for that dinner you owe me. I'm starting to wonder about you."

"How about next –"

Squalo approaches and blurts out to Gloria, "I've been calling you, but you don't answer."

"Hey, Squalo," Gloria replies.

"What does a man need to do to take a lady out for dinner?"

"Squalo, I told you already, we're just friends."

"Yeah, I don't believe –"

Billy cuts him off, "Squalo, we were in the middle of a conversation."

"Oh, excuse me," Squalo sarcastically replies and struts away.

Meanwhile, Belinda gives Blackie a hug to say hello and whispers, "I just heard it's definite, he's getting out."

"I don't want to think about him right now."

While Nutsy and Ladro catch eyes from across the room, Nutsy gives his nod. Ladro nods and heads toward the back door.

Belo approaches Nutsy and asks, "You have a minute?"

"What do ya want, Belo?"

"Look, I know I fucked up."

"Ya sure did." Nutsy strolls away without waiting for Belo's reply.

Bono nervously enters and glances around the room searching for Sammy. He knows his uncle is probably around but is anxious to see her tonight. Since Sammy's eyes have been glued to the front door wondering if Bono would show, she immediately notices him and happily races over. "I'm glad you came."

Bono is excited but appears nervous while searching around for his uncle. Sammy notices Bono's discomfort and says, "Don't worry. You can be my date for tonight."

Belo sees Bono by the front door and races over. "What are you doing here?"

So Bono glances toward Sammy and hesitantly replies, "I'm Sammy's date tonight." Sammy and Bono can't help but smile at each other since they both have what happened this afternoon still on their minds.

"Didn't I tell you to stay –"

Sammy cuts in, "It's my fault. I asked him if he would be my date. Please let him stay for a while."

Belo glances back and forth at Sammy and Bono. This is just fantastic, he thinks, but he reluctantly nods yes and walks away. He can't say no to Sammy.

The other members of The Quad stroll in and all heads turn since they haven't been seen together in public in years. Most residents know they pull the strings in this city.

The Pope approaches Nutsy and says, "Nuccio, it's been awhile." They exchange a handshake.

"How ya been?"

"Good… you got a minute?"

"Yeah, let's go upstairs."

So Nutsy and The Pope head up the staircase. Nutsy opens the door and they both enter The Headquarters and take a seat on a couch by the pool table. "Wow, I haven't been up here in years. It looks marvelous."

"Yeah, a few updates here and there. Ya look good."

"I feel good, how about you?"

"I've felt better. So what's up?"

"I'm concerned about some news circulating around town."

"Like what?"

"For starters, this fixed bet that could destroy you."

"Well, we'll see what happens."

"And this news about The Lion."

Meanwhile, Billy and Gloria are laughing it up by the bar. Squalo keeps on peering towards them with a pissed off look. He's been trying to date Gloria for years, since he knows she's loaded.

Gloria tries to avoid eye contact with Squalo but looks toward him and whispers to Billy, "There's something wrong with that guy."

"Just forget about him," Billy replies.

Nutsy paces back and forth in The Headquarters and says, "Count me out this time."

"Who else in this city got the balls to do it?" The Pope asks.

"Get your brother's family from the island, or the Solders from Da Bronx to do the dirty work."

"Once we go to the outside, all control of this city is given up. You know that."

"This is different though."

"It ain't different. Besides, you know inside these four square miles, heads turn the other way if it helps keep the streets clean. They both gotta go. It's all there is to it."

Nutsy stares for a moment and replies, "It ain't that simple anymore. We're in different times. Cameras are all over the fuckin' place."

"And what's this about Squalo backing you into a corner?"

"Who'd ya hear this from?"

Now Sammy and Bono are happily gazing into each other's eyes in the back of the bar. The afternoon seemed to have changed the direction of their friendship. N-J approaches them and asks, "Is this your boyfriend, Sammy?"

Sammy gives Bono a grin and replies, "No, N-J, we're just good friends right now."

Bono offers his hand to N-J for a handshake and says, "I've heard a lot about you, N-J."

N-J shakes his hand and replies, "She's my sister." N-J was always protective of her.

Bono replies, "I know. And I heard you've always been a great brother."

Nutsy and The Pope are still having their conversation upstairs. "I don't care. That night has been erased from my mind," Nutsy says.

"Fair enough, but this predicament with Leo is a real concern going forward for the both of us."

"He's got nothin' to do with my gig."

"You honestly don't think they know Billy is the puppeteer around here?"

"Billy's done. He's out, retired."

The Pope gives a smile and replies, "Okay, Nutsy, you keep telling yourself that."

Ladro slides down on a thick rope onto Squalo's terrace from the rooftop. Squalo has the top floor so it's a piece of cake for Ladro even with a bum leg since the drop is only around ten feet.

All the pain killers he took earlier are kicking in and definitely helping right now. The real test will be climbing back up the rope since he will be primarily using upper body strength. It's a good thing he's been steadily doing push-ups every night.

Ladro still has his black outfit on with a black ski mask and black gloves. A duffle bag is tied to his waste. He inspects the slider and notices an alarm trigger on one side, the side that obviously slides opens.

He slides out the long, slim piece of metal from inside his jacket and jambs it in the frame that remains closed and doesn't have an alarm trigger.

He maneuvers the metal bar back and forth attempting to pop open the slider. Finally, after a minute of prying, the slider door gives way and he is able to slide it open enough to slip into the apartment.

This was a trick he had done over and over back in the day. Once the stationary side of the slider slips open without the alarm trigger, a thief has full access and the alarm on the door could never trip.

Ladro makes his way to the safe in the dining room and yanks out the drill from the duffle bag and drills a few tiny holes through the safe door.

After a while of drilling and hack sawing, Ladro is able to pop open the safe door. He removes all the piles of cash and packs it tightly into the duffle bag and the inside of his jacket.

A great feature that no one can tell is the inside of Ladro's jacket has large pockets. It's a perfect place for a thief to inconspicuously hide small items. He used this jacket years back when he raided meat freezers in supermarkets.

To break Squalo's balls, Ladro places a rubber shark in the safe and swings the door shut. He's not done though. Nutsy had asked for one more request. So Ladro walks over toward the shark tank and places the tip of the drill bit against the bottom of the tank.

He slowly presses the button on the drill and the bit starts to penetrate the thick glass eventually making its way all the way through.

He carefully pulls the bit back out from the glass and a slow stream of water trickles down the side of the tank and drips onto the floor.

Ladro makes his way out of the apartment and grabs the rope that's hanging from the rooftop.

He slowly yanks himself up the side of the wall, pull by pull. He pauses to catch his breath while only halfway up. "Shit. Let's go," he whispers to himself.

He hears a slider a few apartments away grind open and a couple walk out onto their terrace laughing while holding wine glasses. Fuck, he thinks to himself.

He continues pulling himself slowly up the rope. Since he's attempting to be extremely quiet, it's causing him extra work and his arms burn with tightness. He peeks over toward the couple who are now romantically kissing and thinks, Jesus Christ, can't you go screw inside for a minute.

He's finally able to latch onto the edge of the roof and then hoists himself up. He lies on the roof for a minute while attempting to catch his breath and thinks, shit, boy am I out of shape. Thank God I've been doing pushups.

Ladro looks back over the edge toward the couple and whispers to himself, "Alright, now you can screw each other."

As Nutsy and The Pope head downstairs from The Headquarters, The Pope says, "Look, Nutsy, I thought you knew all this."

"We'll finish this conversation another time."

Nutsy and The Pope separate and head in different directions. Blackie approaches Nutsy and asks, "Have you seen Ladro around?"

"Knowin' that guy, he's probably takin' a shit or something." Nutsy tries to cover up for Ladro.

"That must be some shit."

"He told me his stomach was botherin' him."

"I can't believe these three guys showed up."

"Why, the food is paid for already."

Ladro drives south on the B-R parkway with the radio cranking and a grin from ear to ear. All he can think about is what a score this is. He can't believe he pulled it off. Maybe I got out too soon, he thinks. At the least, this will put me on the map forever one day.

Munchie is pounding down drink after drink. Belinda always wanted their relationship to be private for her own personal reasons, but after Squalo had called Munchie out on their relationship, Munchie insisted they go as a couple.

He knows he's been purposely playing into Belinda's insecurity and wants it to be known he cares for her. Right now, a lot of mixed emotions are flowing through Belinda's mind. The fact that she is with a big time local doctor and not of the same education, or even any education for that matter, gives her an uneasy feeling.

Squalo approaches them and sarcastically asks, "So, tonight you're a couple, ha?"

Belinda replies, "What's that supposed to mean?"

"We'll see about tomorrow," Squalo replies as he struts away.

With an annoyed look, Belinda watches her father strut away. She is not thrilled with her father's comment and knows it was a dig toward them.

"Just ignore him," Munchie says while noticing her irritation.

"It's easy for you to say, I've been dealing with him my whole life."

Nutsy approaches Billy and Gloria by the bar. "Excuse me, Billy, ya got a minute?" Nutsy has a few things on his mind to discuss after his conversation with The Pope.

Billy nods yes and says to Gloria, "I'll be right back."

Nutsy and Billy take a seat at the conference table in The Headquarters and Nutsy says, "You two look chipper."

"What can I say? So what's up?"

"I need ya to be straight with me."

"About what?"

"Are ya still involved with The Quad?"

"What makes you ask me that?" Billy's just trying to gather his thoughts without committing.

"Ya want me to be straight with you all the time, but ya haven't been straight with me."

Billy hesitantly replies, "We needed to discuss a few city things."

"I guess that's when ya BUMPED into The Pope in Fleetville, right?"

While in a heated argument, the barmaid and Vito are now standing outside on the sidewalk in front of Sista. "Ya didn't tell me this was for Nutsy's family," Vito says.

"Why does it matter? You're with me," the barmaid replies.

"Are ya nuts? I can't go in there."

Sammy and Bono decide they need some fresh air. So they both head toward the front door. N-J is always protective of his little sister, so he follows behind them.

Sammy and Bono both step outside and overhear the argument between Vito and the barmaid. Bono doesn't want any issues since his uncle is around and whispers to Sammy, "Let's go back in."

N-J stands inside by the large glass window curiously glancing at Sammy and Bono.

Sammy doesn't care that Vito is around and replies, "Let me cool down first." Not that she really needs to, but she is not fazed by Vito one bit and wants him to know it.

So now Vito looks over toward them both and becomes the wise-ass he usually is. "I always wondered who does who?"

The barmaid replies, "Vito, knock it off!"

Sammy replies, "You'll always be –"

Bono finally gets up some nerve and cuts Sammy off. "You really think you're tough because you're a Lord, don't you?"

Sammy can't believe Bono has finally spoken up. Maybe all the training they have recently completed together is finally giving him some confidence.

"I'm tough anyway," Vito replies.

Sammy can't help but laugh and responds, "You didn't look too tough the other night lying on your back."

The barmaid cuts in, "Let's just leave." She never knew Vito was a Lord and is not thrilled with it.

"Don't tell me what to fucking do," Vito snaps back.

Sammy says, "Don't talk to her like that."

N-J is still glancing out of the window. Although the room is noisy, he can somewhat hear the escalating voices outside and it's making him feel uneasy.

He notices Sammy becoming heated by her body language and starts clutching his fists. N-J notices a knife on one of the tables and slips it up his sleeve.

Bono and Vito are now face to face. Although he knows his uncle is inside, Bono feels like he needs to step-up and be the one to confront Vito. His feelings for Sammy have changed and he needs to show her he can handle himself.

The barmaid yanks on Vito's arm and says, "I work here God Damnit. Stop it now!" As she attempts to yank Vito away, Vito's able to break free from her grip and the force tosses her onto the ground.

While Sammy makes a move toward Vito, the front door flies open and N-J charges out. Sammy notices and yells, "N-J, get back inside!"

Vito violently shoves Bono away who crashes into Sammy and they both stumble backwards.

The knife slips down N-J's wrist and he charges at Vito. Sammy notices and yells, "No!"

While N-J holds the blade out and charges to jab Vito with it, Sammy lunges forward in front of N-J to stop him. The knife accidentally penetrates Sammy's bicep and she hunches over in pain. "Ahhhhhh."

N-J can't believe what he had done and drops the knife and covers his face with his hands. "I'm sorry, Sammy. I'm sorry, Sammy."

The front door of Sista flies open and Blackie storms out. "What the hell's going on?"

Vito bolts down the street since he knows he's way outnumbered and yells, "That wasn't me!"

The barmaid nervously embraces Sammy who is still hunched over in pain and notices blood on the cement sidewalk. She can't believe what had just happened.

Blackie squats down by Sammy and asks, "What happened?"

No one says a word and Blackie becomes agitated. "I asked, what the fuck happened?!"

"It was me. I did it," N-J frantically blurts out. He nervously covers his face. "I'm so sorry, Sammy."

Sammy knows her brother is upset and tries to calm his nerves. Although she is in tremendous pain at this moment, Sammy stands back up and says, "I'm fine, N-J. I'm okay."

Blood now rolls down her bicep, but she does her best to not show N-J the pain she is currently in. She knows this would cause him to become even more upset, and if so, anything could happen.

Blackie gets a feeling that this has something to do with N-J since she has witnessed his behavior before. She notices the knife on the ground by his feet and picks it up.

N-J frantically yells out, "I cut her. I cut my sister." N-J's nerves are rattled.

Sammy knows it and hugs N-J tightly. "Calm down, I'm okay. Calm down." She is doing her best to not show N-J the intense pain she is currently in.

While noticing blood rolling down Sammy's arm, N-J begins to hyperventilate. Sammy looks him in the eyes and calmly says, "Take a deep breath. Just relax."

Kathy charges out from the bar with a concerned look and asks, "What's going on?"

"It was me. It's my fault, I hurt Sammy," N-J blurts out since he can't control his emotions right now.

Kathy notices the knife in Blackie's hand and immediately thinks N-J has something to do with this situation.

Blackie replies, "No it wasn't. She tripped and cut her arm on glass. That's the story." Blackie glares at them all to make sure they understand where she is coming from. "You all got it?"

Kathy replies, "N-J, get back inside, and don't say a word to anyone." Kathy knows exactly what Blackie is attempting to do. The last thing she would want, is N-J to get tangled up with the local police.

Kathy inspects the gash on Sammy's bicep and sees that the knife didn't seem to penetrate too far in.

Blackie glances toward the barmaid and asks, "What was that punk doing here?"

She hesitantly replies, "We started dating about a week ago."

"He's bad news, just so you know," Blackie replies.

Nutsy charges out and asks, "What the fuck's going on out here? N-J's a mess inside."

Blackie replies, "Everything's taken care of."

"Why the fuck is Sammy's arm covered in blood then?" Nutsy glances toward Bono and asks, "Did you have anything to do with this?"

Sammy cuts in, "No, dad, it wasn't him. It was that guy Vito."

"What the fuck is he doing here?" Nutsy's getting charged up.

"He was my date. I'm so sorry, Nutsy," the barmaid replies.

"That's the guy ya asked me if you could bring?"

The barmaid just nods yes. She feels awful right now.

"Let me see this thing." Nutsy inspects the gash. He's seen worse. "Why is your brother cryin' inside?"

"She fell and cut her arm, Nutsy. I'm taking her for stitches. Leave it at that," Blackie says.

Nutsy notices the blade in Blackie's hand and asks, "Did N-J have that?"

Sammy replies, "It was an accident, dad."

"I'm checking on him." Kathy races back into the bar.

"Let's go!" Blackie says to Sammy and Bono as she heads in the direction of the hospital. Sammy and Bono both follow.

The barmaid nervously says to Nutsy, "It wasn't N-J's fault. My date got him nervous."

"We'll talk about this tomorrow. Go have a drink and relax."

So Nutsy races back in and heads toward Kathy and N-J who are at the side of the room. "I know you're upset. Whatever ya did, just forget about it."

"I hurt her, Papa. I hurt Sammy."

Kathy responds, "It was an accident. Listen to your aunt. If anyone asks you anything, Sammy tripped and cut her arm on the sidewalk."

"But you told me to never lie."

While Kathy looks toward Nutsy hoping for his assistance with this matter, Nutsy replies, "Papa's telling ya just this time, alright?"

N-J glances toward Kathy for her approval and she nods yes. So N-J nods and replies, "Are you mad at me?"

"No, but we will be if ya don't say she tripped," Nutsy replies.

Ladro slips in through the back door beaming from ear to ear. He has no idea what just happened outside and pours a healthy celebratory drink at the bar.

Nutsy approaches Munchie and Belinda by the bar and asks, "Belinda, can I have a word with you?"

So Belinda nods and follows Nutsy to a private corner and he asks, "This new kid Vito that works with you, what's his deal?"

"He's a low-level wannabe from The Hills, why?"

"He's been causing a lot of problems around here."

"He's definitely a troublemaker, but that's about it."

"I've known ya for a while. Either talk to him or I will."

"He's not my problem after tomorrow."

"Why?"

"My brother's taking over. I'm getting pushed down."

Nutsy stares without a word.

CHAPTER 20

Blackie, Sammy, and Bono are now sitting in the emergency room. While a doctor tends to Sammy's cut, he says to her, "It's not terrible... I have to report this though since it was a stabbing."

Blackie asks with a serious tone, "Report what? There's nothing to report."

"Any gunshot or stab wounds are automatic."

"Didn't you read the report? It was from glass on a sidewalk," Blackie replies.

"I didn't notice any traces of glass in the cut and it seems pretty clear cut to me."

"I think you better take another look at this closely. My brother's not going to be happy."

So, the doctor notices the name on the clipboard and asks, "Are you related to Nuccio Gento?"

"He's my father," Sammy replies.

"And also happens to be my brother," Blackie replies.

The doctor stares at Blackie for a moment in thought. He glances toward Bono and asks, "Were you there?"

"Yes, that's exactly what happened."

Blackie says with a serious tone, "I'm sure you can find a spec in there somewhere, isn't that right, doc?"

All Sammy can think about is what a smooth operator her aunt is. Since the doctor knows Nutsy's reputation, he nods yes to go along with the story. After all, Nutsy's also a major contributor to the hospital and the doctor knows it.

Blackie's cell phone rings and she answers, "We're good."

Kathy is on the other end and asks, "What about N-J?"

"It's being taken care of as we speak."

Nutsy is now wound up and enters The Headquarters to finish his conversation with Billy. "I thought you forgot about me," Billy says.

Nutsy doesn't want to mention what just happened so he replies, "I had to take care of a few things." Nutsy knows Billy would get extremely angry at N-J since he always reminds him to stay away from the knives.

"Is Gloria alright?" Billy asks.

"She's fine."

"Look, Nutsy, I know you're annoyed but this new law screwed everything up. I really thought you'd be long gone by the time he got out."

Nutsy heats up a little and replies, "Is this why you've been bustin' my balls to get out, to cover your own ass?"

"Own ass? Why, a father-in-law looking after his only son? I did this for you and Kathy, and I won't apologize for it."

"I'm not askin' for an apology. I'm askin' why I was never told this."

"We all do things that aren't always told, don't we?"

"Where is this heading now?"

"That night with Papo, thirty years ago, did I ever question you when you told me you weren't involved?"

Nutsy hesitantly replies, "No."

"That's right no. Whatever happened that night saved this city, so no one gave a shit, not even the police. You were dating my daughter at the time and friends kept asking me if you were involved."

Nutsy just stares without a word.

"I never pressed you about it. I knew exactly why it was done. The Westerns would have the reigns right now, and you'd be working for Squalo and Leo if I didn't do what I did."

"We're talkin' about apples and oranges here."

"How about we call it what it is and leave it at that? I'm going back downstairs." Billy walks out.

Approximately thirty years ago, The Pope owned a bowling alley in the northern part of the city. A violent group from the west side of Manhattan was attempting to take over The Vern. They made frequent visits to The Vern and purposely disrupted local merchants and wreaked havoc on the streets.

It was a troubling time for both the residents and the local police force.

This group was notorious for taking over small villages and cities by using fear and violence. They stopped at nothing until they achieved their goals.

They were using the bowling alley as their base when they visited The Vern. One night, The Pope purposely closed the bowling alley to residents and only allowed The Westerns in.

They were drinking and plotting their next moves, when two masked, gunman charged out from the back of the alley and opened fire dropping all ten of The Westerns like ducks in a barrel.

When the cops arrived at the gruesome scene, no one saw a thing, so they say. Since the cops were all glad to see this violent group finally wiped out, they never pressed on with an investigation and kept it quiet.

To this day, it's still a mystery about the shooters, but most could put two and two together. That was around the time Nutsy earned his nickname although he always denied he took part in it. This has never been brought up again until now.

Squalo approaches Gloria by the bar and says, "Maybe I can get a few words in now."

Although Gloria can't stand him, she doesn't want to seem rude and asks, "How has The Plains been treating you?"

"Okay, for the time being."

Gloria knows exactly what he means but brushes it off. "Where are you heading, down south?"

"I guess you can say that. Hey, I always wondered, was it unanimous or a split decision?"

"I'm not sure what you're asking me."

"You know, the vote that pushed me out. Which way did you go?"

"I have no idea what you're talking about." Gloria becomes uncomfortable and searches around for Billy.

"Don't you find it ironic about this city, that no one ever knows what the other person is talking about?"

Billy finally arrives and can tell by Gloria's stare she is not thrilled that Squalo is around.

So Squalo sarcastically says, "Here he is, the best-looking man in town." Squalo has been drinking and is ready to stir up the night.

In the past, Billy has witnessed Squalo's behavior when he's been drinking and replies, "It looks like you've had enough, Squalo."

Squalo blows off Billy's comment and asks, "Whoever named it The Quad? It sounds like some rodeo event or something like that."

Billy and Gloria catch eyes. They both know Squalo is breaking horns.

Squalo sarcastically asks, "How do I become a member of this elite group of fine individuals?"

Billy replies, "We'll give you an application, how about that?" Billy is getting tired of listening to his bullshit.

"Hold onto it. I probably won't need it," Squalo replies and struts away.

After finishing up at the hospital, Blackie, Sammy, and Bono head back toward Sista. Luckily, she only needed a few stitches. The doctor did finally agree to Blackie's story since it wasn't as bad as he thought, and knew, he didn't have much of a choice.

A group of derelicts stand on a dark corner tilting back drinks in brown paper bags. Blackie notices them and whispers, "Just keep walking and don't make eye contact."

As they pass the derelicts, one sarcastically yells out, "Shit, look at the asses on these two hoes."

While they continue passing by, another man yells out, "Damn, I'd even pay a hundred for a B-J."

Blackie turns and says, "Sure, that sounds fine." She whispers to Sammy and Bono, "Stay here."

"Aunt Blackie, forget it," Sammy whispers back.

Blackie approaches the derelicts and asks, "Which asshole is it?"

"Whoa!" A few men say to instigate.

A rough looking man moves in front of the pack and asks, "Who are you calling an asshole?"

"Who are you calling a hoe?" Blackie asks while staring straight into his eyes.

Another man asks, "Aren't you Nutsy's sister?"

"No," Blackie replies. The comments set her off and she removes her high heels.

"Dude, this is Nutsy's sister. Drop it." He recognizes Blackie since he's one of Nutsy's clients.

"I guess tonight's your lucky night," the man says sarcastically.

Blackie laughs it off and replies, "You're right. If my niece wasn't here, I'd be in jail for ramming your head in the concrete sidewalk." Blackie walks away.

"Whoa! Oh shit," the derelicts say.

"You come back any time," the man says.

"I plan on it." Blackie meets up with Sammy and Bono. "Let's go."

Sammy says, "You're crazy for doing this." The funny thing is, they both act the same way and then question each other about their actions later.

"There's one thing about men. They all have big mouths until you call them out… don't ever do this though." Blackie laughs as they continue heading back toward Sista.

Nutsy stands in the middle of the room trying to take it all in. A lot has happened tonight. I'm supposed to be just enjoying this party and not thinking about all this bullshit, he thinks.

Kathy walks up to him and says, "You look lost."

"Ya hear from Blackie?"

"Yeah, they're on their way back. It wasn't as bad as it looked."

"What about the other thing?"

"The doctor brushed it off. Thank God. That could've been an issue with his place."

Nutsy gazes around. His mind is spinning.

"What's the matter?" Kathy asks.

"Nothing, ya wouldn't understand anyway."

The drawings Kathy found in Nutsy's dresser drawer have been on her mind all night, so she asks, "What are the sketches about?"

"What sketches?"

"The ones that are tucked under your socks."

"What are ya going through my shit now?"

"Who do you think puts your laundry away?"

"It's just somethin' I play around with from time to time, to take my mind off of things."

Nutsy catches eyes with Ladro at the bar who gives him a nod. Nutsy knows the job is complete. Ladro shoots back a shot glass.

"Does this have anything to do with your dream?" Kathy curiously asks.

Nutsy doesn't reply and catches Ladro shooting back another shot.

"I knew it had to do with N-J. I just knew it," Kathy continues on.

Nutsy remains quiet.

"It's okay if you show emotion, once in a while."

"That's easy for you to say."

Blackie, Sammy, and Bono enter Sista. N-J has been impatiently waiting for Sammy and bolts over toward her. "I'm sorry. Do you forgive me?" N-J wraps his arms around her.

"N-J, you didn't do it on purpose. Just forget it already," Sammy replies.

Squalo and Donnola approach Nutsy and Kathy and Squalo says, "Beautiful party. We're heading out." He glances toward Nutsy and asks, "We're still on for six-thirty tomorrow?"

"Unless you're not showing up?"

"I wouldn't miss it for the world." Squalo and Donnola move away. Donnola doesn't shake hands or even say thank you like the weasel he is.

"Fuckin' rodent," Nutsy mumbles as he moves toward the bar.

Kathy yells out to Nutsy, "Where are you going? We didn't finish our conversation."

"It's a dead issue," Nutsy replies as he heads towards Ladro by the bar. "How did it go?"

"Like I said before, I wouldn't leave a piece of dust in that fucking thing."

"What about the tank?"

"It's dripping as we speak."

Belo sees Nutsy and Ladro together at the bar and decides to take this opportunity to speak with them. He's feeling pretty good also. "It's a great party, Nutsy. Thank you for inviting me," Belo says.

Nutsy doesn't respond or look his way.

"Come on already. How do I make this right?"

So Nutsy has enough of Belo asking and says, "Ya wanna make this right, take The Lion down when he gets out."

They stare at each other for a moment. Belo glances toward Ladro who gives him his standard shrug like, don't look at me for help.

CHAPTER 21

Squalo and Donnola are now driving north on the main avenue approaching the roundabout. Squalo spins the steering wheel and says, "It's about time they put this thing back. The traffic was a fucking mess here."

Squalo's cell phone rings through the Bluetooth and he answers, "Squalo!"

Squalo's building manager is standing in the apartment below Squalo's and asks, "Are you close by?"

"Who is this?"

"The building manager."

"I'm about a half hour away, why?"

The manager glances up at the ceiling which has water stains with some areas already leaking. "You might have a broken pipe. The ceiling below yours is dripping."

"What?!"

"Hurry up and get here."

"Fuck." Squalo presses a button on the dashboard and says, "You gotta take a ride. I might have an issue at the apartment."

Carmela approaches Billy and Gloria at the bar and says, "If I didn't know any better, I'd swear you two are lovebirds."

Gloria laughs and replies, "It's so nice to see you again, Carmela. How's Florida treating you?"

"You have to come down and visit."

"I'd love that." Gloria eyes Billy and asks, "How about we both visit her?"

Billy smiles and replies, "I'm sure we can arrange something."

It's twelve o'clock and the party is nearing the end but first, coffee and cake need to be served. Kathy stands in the middle of the room with two cakes, one for N-J and one for Carmela.

As the guests sing happy birthday, N-J flashes a beaming smile. Kathy can't be excited enough for him and stands next to him as he blows out his candles.

Kathy glances toward Nutsy and can only think about the sketches she found. She knows down deep inside Nutsy has mixed feelings but would never show it. Maybe he wants this sports complex to be about N-J, or maybe, about kids with autism, she thinks.

While the guests cheer after N-J blows out his candles, Nutsy hugs him tightly and says, "I love ya, pal."

"Love you too, papa."

Belo and Linda catch eyes. She is still pissed off at Belo and asks, "This is what you gave up for those fucking assholes?" Linda walks away.

Belo approaches Ladro who is standing next to Blackie and whispers in his ear, "Let's just hit the safe, you and me." Belo is desperate to make good. He wants no part of Leo and knows this is already causing issues with his wife.

"Forget it. It ain't worth it. I got enough problems right now." Ladro plays it off.

Kathy places another cake onto the table and the guests sing happy birthday to Carmela. Gloria whispers into Billy's ear, "Your place or mine?"

"This could change our friendship, you know?"

Gloria replies, "I hope it does." They smile at each other.

Munchie appears to be a complete mess. Besides guzzling drinks all night, he is extremely nervous about his current dilemma and it shows. He wonders how he got caught in the middle of all this.

Nutsy has been avoiding him all night and for good reason. Since Nutsy decided to book all of Munchie's bets and either keep the cash or return it, he now knows he should be able to make good even if the fix is true. Plus, Ladro has the money from the safe. The tide is turning.

Squalo and Donnola race down the hallway toward Squalo's apartment. The manager has been eagerly waiting for him to arrive and is standing outside his apartment door.

Squalo slides his key in the doorknob and says, "It can't be from my apartment, everything was fine when I left."

So Squalo pushes open the door and they head into the apartment. As they get closer toward the dining room, Donnola notices water on the floor and says, "Yup... looks like it's from here."

Squalo looks down and says, "What the fuck?"

The manager sees the water dripping down the side of the shark tank and says, "It looks like it's from the tank."

Squalo races toward the shark tank which is now currently half empty. He bends down and notices the small drill hole toward the bottom of the tank and then nervously peeks toward the safe.

A picture covers the safe on the wall so Squalo races over and quickly removes the picture. "Mother fucker!" He swings open the door and pulls out the rubber shark from the empty safe.

Donnola's eyes open wide and he nervously asks, "Please tell me you didn't get hit?"

The manager says, "Look, I don't know what's going on here, but I have to address the water issue."

"Water issue?! There was seven-fifty in this fucking thing and you think I'm concerned about a little water?"

The manager's eyes open wide and he asks, "Were you just robbed?"

"How the fuck could I get robbed with the alarm on?"

So Squalo races over toward the slider and sees the stationary door slightly open. He notices the door that slides open has not been touched and is still secure.

He glances toward Donnola with an irate look and asks, "Was that fucking asshole there all night?"

"I think so."

"Jesus Christ. We let our guard down."

"Hey, you were more concerned about busting balls all night."

"Oh, now it's my fault?"

The manager says, "I have to get a bucket and report the robbery to the front desk."

Squalo replies, "You keep your mouth shut. You got me?"

"You don't want this reported?"

"How do I explain I have seven-hundred and fifty-grand in a fucking wall safe?"

The manager nods and walks away. He knows what Squalo is mixed up in since he's a player himself and doesn't press the issue.

Squalo stares down at the mess. "Look at this. My whole wood floor is wrecked. What the fuck am I gonna do with the sharks now?"

"You better find something to plug up the hole or stick them in the bathtub."

"It's saltwater you idiot." Squalo is fired up.

The party is just about ending and Munchie's cell phone rings displaying Squalo's name and he answers, "What's up, Squalo?"

"Did you give my fucking code out to anyone?" Squalo is livid.

Munchie looks toward Ladro who is now laughing it up at the bar with Nutsy and replies, "Of course not, why?"

"Is Belo still there?"

"Yeah, I think he's leaving soon."

"Put him on!"

Munchie nervously hands Belo the phone. "It's Squalo."

So Belo answers, "Yeah?"

"Did you give my fucking code to anyone?"

"What are you talking about? Munchie never gave it to me."

Squalo hesitantly replies, "The safe got cleaned out."

"What?!" Belo quickly peeks over toward Ladro. They catch eyes but Ladro turns away and shoots back a shot. "All of it?" Belo nervously asks.

"No, just a crumb… of course all of it. Put that asshole on."

"Nutsy or Ladro?"

"The thief, you fucking moron!"

Belo hands off the phone to Ladro and says with a concerned look, "It's Squalo. He said the safe was hit tonight."

Nutsy yells out, "Are you fuckin' kiddin' me?!"

So Ladro answers, "Asshole, don't you have an alarm?"

"You better pray I don't find out it was you," Squalo snaps back.

"Go fuck yourself, Squalo." Ladro tosses the phone to Belo.

Nutsy grabs the phone from Belo and says, "I don't give a shit what happened, ya better make good on my money."

"We all took it up the ass," Squalo replies.

"Not me." Nutsy tosses the phone to Belo.

Squalo hangs up the phone and says, "What a perfect night, ha? Fucking party going on, everyone feeling good… was that bitch there all night?"

Donnola shrugs.

Nutsy asks Belo, "How many people knew that code?"

"Just Munchie."

"Munchie, get over here!" Nutsy yells out.

Kathy and Blackie have been listening to the ruckus and Blackie whispers, "I fucking knew it."

"You know what's going on?" Kathy asks.

As Blackie and Ladro catch eyes, Blackie replies to Kathy, "We'll talk later."

Munchie nervously says to the guys, "I swear I have nothing to do with it."

Belo says, "This is just great. No one knows anything and we're each out a buck eighty-seven."

CHAPTER 22

It's about fifteen minutes later and the manager arrives back at Squalo's apartment with a mop and large pail. He does his best to plug up the hole with silicon for the time being to prevent any further water damage.

Squalo eventually drove Donnola home and currently sits in his living room staring at the slider in thought. He knows whoever did this knew exactly what they were doing and that the safe was stuffed with cash.

He wonders if Ladro could have pulled this off with a bum leg. Maybe it was Blackie or even Munchie for that matter. But if they had the code, why would they drill the door of the safe open? Squalo's mind is twirling around in circles.

Maybe they had the code and just made it seem like they didn't. Squalo is a conniver himself and can think up many different scenarios.

Blackie races into her house after arguing with Ladro on the ride home. She confronted him about the safe, but he continuously denies it. She knows it's too close to the vest and all fingers will point to him. "You can't even be straight with me," Blackie says while she kicks off her high heels.

"How many times I gotta say it? It wasn't me."

"I noticed you were gone for a while. Where were you?"

"Upstairs, tallying up the numbers for the week."

Nutsy and his family wander into their house. Kathy is extremely happy with the night except for the incident with Sammy.

Sammy is fine and that's all that matters to her right now. She has her family all together and wants to take in every moment she can until N-J goes back.

Nutsy nods toward Sammy and says, "Ya got your first battle scars, ha?"

"I guess you can say that."

"How does it feel?"

"I'm fine, like it never happened."

"Yeah, what else would ya say?"

Carmela says, "She's a warrior, Nutsy, just like her aunt."

"Yeah, I know. That's the problem."

Kathy replies, "You should be glad."

"Yeah, I'm ecstatic," Nutsy sarcastically replies as he strolls into the living room and pours a drink.

Ladro is in his living room having a night cap. He can't believe he just made the score of a lifetime. Now he just needs to get away with it.

Blackie races in wearing a nightgown and says, "I knew it was never out of your system. You just had to do it, right?"

"Are we starting this shit again?"

"Always playing dumb, that's all you do... while even knowing his son's getting out."

"They can both go fuck themselves for all I care."

"You don't know this guy like I do."

"I'm sure I don't."

"You're a fucking moron, you know that? I'm going to bed." Blackie races out.

"I'll be in after I finish."

"Don't do me any favors," Blackie replies from the foyer.

It's around six-thirty in the morning and Squalo's eyes slowly open while sitting in the same chair he had fallen asleep in the night before. He stands up and attempts to straighten out his stiff back and neck.

He wanders into the kitchen and presses a button on his coffee maker. He notices the rubber shark sitting on his counter and mumbles, "Yeah, real funny. Your time will come."

It's about eight o'clock in the morning and Squalo is driving to the state jail to finally pick up Leo. He presses a button on the dashboard and waits for his insurance agent to answer.

A man's voice sounds through the car's speakers. "This can't be good."

Squalo replies, "It's not... Presto, I think I have to tear up all my floors."

"Why?"

"My tank leaked last night and dripped all over the place."

"Are you kidding me?"

"Would I be calling this early if I was?"

"I guess not... what happened?"

"It must've cracked or something."

Presto hesitates for a moment and Squalo asks, "Are you still there?"

"Yeah... it's probably not covered, Squalo."

"What are you talking about? Isn't this why I pay for insurance?"

"Yeah, but the policy doesn't cover when things crack on their own."

"So, when is it covered?"

"Things like fire, broken pipes, theft, wind damage."

Squalo heats up and asks, "So if I burn this whole building down, you'll cover me then?"

Presto laughs while Squalo continues on, "Yeah, keep laughing. Just figure it out." Squalo presses the button on the dashboard to hang up the call. "Nothing's ever covered with these fucking crooks."

It's about an hour later and Squalo sits in his car waiting for the gates to open at the jail house. All he can think about at this time is who could've hit the safe but all fingers still point to one person.

The gate slowly grinds open and Leo comes strutting out with his hair slicked back while wearing faded jeans and a dated T-shirt. He steps passed the gate and pauses. Things seem very different to him, especially the style of the new sleek cars.

While he takes in a deep breath, an officer close by yells out, "Three months is the over under for you and take a guess what I took?"

Leo doesn't acknowledge the officer or even glance his way. He's a free man now. While Squalo approaches him, Leo takes in another deep breath and says, "It smells a lot better on this side of the gate."

Squalo gives Leo a tight hug and replies, "I'm sure it does… you look even bigger in person than behind the glass."

"You work out every day, all day, and you would too."

As they both stroll toward Squalo's car, Leo smirks at the officer and winks just to bust his balls. The officer flips him the bird.

They both slide into Squalo's car and Leo peeks around. The inside of the car looks totally different from what he remembered. "So what's the first thing you'd like to do?" Squalo asks.

"How about getting laid?"

"That I can't help you with."

Leo laughs and replies, "I want a stack of pancakes and French toast. How about we hit a diner?"

So Squalo hits the gas and the Bluetooth rings. Leo is somewhat startled from the sound and asks, "Is that the blue... whatever it's called?"

"Yeah, you got a lot of catching up to do," Squalo replies as he presses the button on the dashboard and answers, "Yeah, what's up?"

"Did you get Leo yet?" Donnola asks while sitting in his messy apartment.

"He's in the car as we speak."

Leo says, "This sounds like the weasel."

"The Lion made it out! Congratulations," Donnola replies.

"I guess these shithead politicians ain't too bad after all, ha?" Leo asks.

Donnola replies, "I guess not. Squalo, how'd you make out with the tank?"

"Would you believe Presto said it might not be covered?"

"Why not?" Donnola asks.

"Do these crooks ever cover anything? I'll call you later."

"Wait… what about the safe?"

"We gotta figure it out. That money can't be too far away." Squalo presses the button to end the call.

"You talk through the stereo speakers now?" Leo asks.

"Like I said, you got a lot of catching up to do."

"What safe is he talking about?" Leo curiously asks.

While Nutsy takes a shower, Kathy curiously pulls out his drawings from under the clothes and gazes at them. She's trying to figure out exactly what he's attempting to sketch. They are rough at best and Nutsy's handwriting isn't the greatest unless it's numbers, of course.

"Kathy!" Nutsy yells from the shower. Kathy nervously tucks the drawings back under his clothes and moves toward the bathroom.

"What is it?" Kathy asks.

"What happened to the shampoo?"

"I'll check the other bathroom. Maybe N-J took it."

CHAPTER 23

Squalo and Leo sit in a local diner in The Plains with empty dishes and glasses in front of them. A cute waitress approaches with a coffee pot and asks, "Any more coffee for either one of you?"

Leo nods yes while giving the waitress a smile. She pours more coffee into his cup and moves away toward the next table. As Leo gazes at her backside, Squalo notices and says, "You look like a dog in heat."

"It's been a while since I saw an ass like that… do you think that dipshit hit your safe?"

"I'm not sure. He's no kid, but it wouldn't surprise me… so what are we doing with Belinda?"

"She can go back on truck duty."

"I don't think she's gonna go for that. She got a taste of the good life."

"That's her problem, not mine… is she seeing anyone?"

"You wouldn't believe it if I told you."

"Who?"

"Munchie."

"Get the fuck outta here! She's with that potato chip eating motherfucker?"

"Apparently so. Don't ask me how."

"Good… I learned a few new medical scams we can use him for. It's easy money."

Vito struts through the diner and Squalo notices. "This is the kid I've been telling you about."

Leo turns and watches as Vito heads toward their table. "He looks like a chump if you ask me."

"Nah, the kid has balls. At the least, he's willing to do the dirty work."

"Well, you know I gotta lay low for a while. They'll have a thousand eyes on me right now."

"This is what I'm saying. We'll let him take the rap if we have to."

Vito shakes hands with Squalo and nods toward Leo. Vito has no idea who Leo is. While Leo just stares without acknowledging him, Squalo says, "This is my son, Leo."

Vito excitedly glances toward Leo and says, "Wow, I can't believe it. You're like a legend around here."

As they shake hands, Leo replies, "Legends are dead. I'm not yet."

"Have a seat," Squalo says. Vito takes a seat and Squalo continues on, "I need you to do something."

"Yeah, what?"

"Tonight, I'm meeting Nutsy and Ladro. I need you to break into Ladro's house and look for cash."

"You want me to break into his house? Fuck that!"

Leo replies, "I told you he looked like a chump." Leo is attempting to bait him.

So Squalo puckers his mouth in a disappointed way and shrugs. Vito can tell they are both not pleased with his answer, so he ponders the idea. He's been excited for the opportunity to work with Leo and knows this could ruin it. The last thing Vito wants is to start off on the wrong foot and hesitantly asks, "What if his wife is home?"

Leo is not thrilled with Vito. "Where did you find this fucking guy, at a toy store?"

"You don't go then. Use some common sense," Squalo snaps back.

Leo says, "That's assuming he has any."

Ladro slides inside one of his kitchen floor cabinets and removes the back panel that's not secured. He reaches into a hole in the sheetrock and pulls out a large stack of money.

He hears footsteps coming from the staircase, so he quickly shoves the stack back into the hole and places the panel back against the wall.

While he slides his body back out from the cabinet, Blackie wanders in and asks, "What are you doing?"

So Ladro stands up and replies, "I thought I heard water dripping under there."

"Really? The sink is on the other side."

"You know these shady contractors. They run pipes all over the place."

"Is that where it is?"

"What?" Ladro attempts to play it off.

Blackie loses her patience and opens the cabinet door and slips her head in. She turns her cell phone light on and peeks around. She notices a gap on the back of the panel and tugs on it. The panel easily falls off. She reaches into the hole and slides out the stack of money.

Ladro can't believe she found the cash and says, "Don't say a word."

So Blackie stands up and asks, "I thought you were upstairs crunching numbers? Whose is it?"

"You're better off not knowing."

"Oh, you're gonna tell me, even if I have to beat it out of you."

It's about a half an hour later and Squalo and Leo are now heading toward the body shop in The Vern. Leo glances toward the bank that Blackie works in and asks, "Blackie still in there?"

"As far as I know."

"Pull over for a minute."

Squalo pulls the car over and says, "It's too early to start any shit."

"Relax… I'll be right back." Leo slips out of the car and struts toward the bank.

He enters the front door and is greeted by a nice young lady in the lobby. "Can I help you?"

"Yeah, I have an appointment with Maria."

"Do you mean Blackie?"

While Leo nods his head yes, the young lady continues and asks, "And your name is, sir?"

"Tell her, Leonardo is here to see her."

"Sure, sir, have a seat."

The young lady enters Blackie's office and says, "Your appointment is here. And he's cute."

"I don't have an appointment until later this afternoon," Blackie replies while sitting at her desk.

"Well, he apparently knows you. He asked for Maria."

Blackie's eyes open wide and she asks, "Did he say his name?"

"Yes, Leonardo."

"Jesus Christ." Blackie stands up and glances out of her office.

"What's wrong?"

"Nothing."

"Should I send him back here?"

Blackie nods yes with an annoyed look.

The young lady approaches Leo in the lobby and says, "She'll see you now. She's in the last office in the back."

Leo stands up and replies, "You're cute, you know that?" Leo smiles and heads toward Blackie's office in the back of the room.

While Blackie sits in her chair watching Leo strut into her office, Leo grins and says, "Life must be treating you well. I remember when you sat at the first desk."

"What do you want, Leo?"

"Well, for starters, I was hoping for a, congratulations. Second, I need to open a bank account."

"There're plenty of banks around."

"I figured it would be easier for you to put in the money your husband still owes me."

"There was no money, Leo. You already know that."

"All I heard about while I was rotting in jail was how the thief made it out with over a hundred grand."

"Rumors mean shit. You should be the first person to understand that."

Leo laughs and replies, "I know you all think I was the trigger man, but you're wrong."

"Well, so are you about the money."

Leo gazes around in thought. He stands up and says, "The lioness is guarding the gazelles, ha?"

"I think you mean the fox is guarding the hen house."

Leo gives a devilish grin and replies, "When you're ready to come back, you know where to find me. And let your husband know I stopped by." Leo struts away without waiting for a reply.

As Leo struts passed the young lady in the lobby, she smiles and says, "Have a nice day."

Leo flashes a smile and winks at her replying, "Thanks beautiful, you too." The young lady blushes.

Leo slides back into the passenger seat of the car and Squalo asks, "You had to go break balls, didn't you?"

"Wow, she still looks good... let's hit the shop now."

Nutsy and Ladro sit at the conference table crunching numbers on a calculator. "How much ya got on the under so far?" Nutsy asks.

"I'm at five-seventy-five."

"Alright, we got a little cushion."

"It wasn't eight, you know. More like six-fifty in that safe."

"Knowing him, he used some of the money to cover his bets. What's the total coming from Munchie?"

Ladro scans a pad and replies, "He's at two-twenty."

"Are ya positive or do I need to check this too?" Nutsy sarcastically asks.

Ladro gets annoyed since Nutsy's still busting his balls about his mixed-up slips and slides the pad in front of Nutsy. "Here, go ahead. Treat me like a fucking three-year-old after all these years."

"Come on, I'm just screwin' around."

"You are and you're not."

"That doesn't even make sense."

"You know exactly what I'm talking about." While Nutsy laughs, Ladro continues, "Just so you know, your sister found the stack of pancakes."

Nutsy leans back and folds his arms. "I thought ya stuck it in the wall?"

"I did. You know her, she's skeptical about everything."

Squalo parks in front of the body shop and says, "This should be interesting."

"She's a big girl. She'll get over it."

As they both slide out of the car and shut the doors, Squalo asks, "You're coming later to meet Nutsy, right?"

"You think I would miss that?"

They both enter the store and Leo notices the young secretary behind the counter and whispers to Squalo, "You never told me how good looking the secretary is."

"Keep it in your pants, will you please."

Leo glances toward the secretary and says, "I'm Leo."

She smiles and replies, "I'm Danielle." She already heard about him and that he'd be showing up soon.

Leo gives a quick wink and heads toward Belinda's office with Squalo. They enter Belinda's office and Leo says, "It's good to see you again, sis."

Belinda stands up from behind her desk and replies, "Leo."

They hug and then take a seat. Belinda already knows where this conversation will be heading and is not thrilled. "How's business been?" Leo asks.

"No problems at all," Belinda replies without any hesitation.

Leo takes a glimpse around the room and notices some feminine decorations. The first thing that goes through his mind is, this is all going. "How many nights is the truck out?" Leo asks.

"Twice, sometimes three, but it's time to give it a rest. It's starting to look suspicious."

This now leads to a different topic. "So, I heard you're seeing Munchie?" Leo asks.

Belinda glares at Squalo with an annoyed look and Squalo just gives her a shrug.

Leo continues, "That's good... we can use him for a few things."

"That's not happening. Your father already got him into a mess."

Squalo cuts in, "Your father? What the hell does that mean?"

"I want you both to leave him alone... and I'm not playing around with this."

"Whoa! My little sis getting bold, I like it."

"Don't call me your little sis. I've been running things for years now, and you come here barking orders just like that?"

"Let's say, you babysat while I was on vacation and now vacation's over."

Belinda glares back toward Squalo. He just shrugs and stays quiet.

Blackie enters The Headquarters and notices Nutsy and Ladro at the conference table still crunching numbers. "Did you tally up the score yet?" Blackie sarcastically asks Ladro since she's still annoyed with him.

Neither Nutsy nor Ladro acknowledge Blackie and continue crunching numbers. The heist is the last thing they would want to discuss with anyone, including her.

Blackie continues, "Yeah, just ignore me now."

"We're not ignoring you, we just need to get the final numbers," Ladro replies.

"Well maybe, this will get your attention. Take a guess who stopped by my bank today?"

Nutsy sarcastically replies, "The fairy godmother."

Ladro replies, "I'm thinking more like Oz."

While they both break out in laughter, Blackie replies with a serious tone, "You're both wrong. Try more like The Lion."

Nutsy and Ladro both look up toward Blackie. "Oh, I guess it ain't funny anymore," Blackie sarcastically says.

It's about a half an hour later and Kathy decides to bring N-J to visit Nutsy at work since N-J's going back in a day or two.

Blackie already headed back to work annoyed since she can tell neither one of them are taking Leo seriously. They figure he's on parole and needs to be calm, but Blackie knows otherwise since she has witnessed his violent behavior in the past.

Kathy and N-J wander into The Headquarters and Ladro says, "Here he is, the greatest pitcher to ever come out of The Vern."

"I wish, Uncle Larry."

"You'll always be the greatest in my book, N-J. I saw you throw gas back in the day."

"Yeah, until they wouldn't let me play anymore," N-J replies with a disappointed look.

Kathy replies, "It was for your own safety, N-J."

"It wasn't right, ma. They said I didn't know how to catch, but I did." N-J gets a little heated.

Nutsy cuts in, "Hey, how about we take a ride and feed the ducks before ya go back?"

"Can we go now?" N-J excitedly asks.

Nutsy peeks at his watch and replies, "Half hour." He glances at Kathy and says, "Grab some Italian loaves from Rotta's. They'll love that bread."

Squalo and Leo are back in the car heading toward The Plains. "She didn't look happy, ha?" Leo asks.

"Nope."

"So, tell me about this safe."

"Unless they hired it out, there's only one person who could've pulled this off... maybe two tops."

"Was there a lot in there?"

"Enough." Squalo doesn't want Leo to know the exact amount. Although Leo is his son, he still doesn't trust him a hundred percent yet, especially with money.

"So, what about the situation between this punk and Nutsy's daughter?"

"I don't know the whole story but apparently she kicked his ass at the bar."

"She kicked his ass?" While Squalo nods yes, Leo shakes his head and asks, "Did anyone back him up?"

"No, I guess they knew she was Nutsy's daughter."

"Did Belinda retaliate yet?"

"Apparently not."

"Well, that's one of the first things we gotta set straight. No one fucks with a Lord."

"That's what happens when you put a woman with a kind heart in charge."

The one thing Squalo hasn't figured out yet is Belinda's agenda for not retaliating.

CHAPTER 24

Nutsy and Kathy are with N-J and stroll across a concrete pathway next to the sound in New Row. It's a peaceful and soothing place with a view of a large body of water and a grassy area to lounge and picnic with family and friends.

As they stroll across this path, Kathy glances around with happy thoughts and asks, "Nutsy, do you remember coming here when the kids were younger and having a barbecue?"

"Yup, sure do. N-J spent all day feeding the ducks."

N-J replies, "I loved doing that when I was younger."

"Those were good times, Kathy. We used to have a feast with like, thirty people here cooking burgers, hot sausage, drinkin' coolers of beer."

N-J rips off a piece of bread from the Italian loaf and chucks it into the water. A few ducks swim over. "Dad, did you ever notice the difference between when Houston plays at home or away?"

"What do you mean?"

"Their batting averages are much higher at home. Check it out."

"How do ya know?"

"I read the stats in the magazines. It's a proven fact."

"Maybe they're just more comfortable hittin' in their own stadium," Nutsy replies.

"Yeah, maybe, but it's a pretty big difference."

Kathy says, "I'm not following you."

"You wouldn't understand anyway, ma."

"I know baseball just as well as you two. Who do you think sat in the bleachers and watched every game when you played years back?"

"Oh yeah, ma. If you have two strikes and you bunt a ball foul, what is it?"

"You could at least give me something a little harder than that."

Nutsy replies, "Let it be, N-J, you're embarrassing her."

"I'm not embarrassed at all… you're out."

N-J smiles and replies, "You're right, ma."

"I know I'm right." Kathy gives Nutsy a look.

It's about a half an hour later and Nutsy, Kathy, and N-J are driving back toward The Vern. "Hey, I have a good idea. How about we stop for some clams and buttered corn?" Nutsy asks.

"If it's where I think, I love their corn," N-J excitedly replies from the backseat.

Kathy says, "Wow, we haven't been there in years."

Carmela and Sammy are eating lunch in the kitchen and having a heart to heart conversation about her future. "You have to follow your dreams, Sammy. Your father will get over it."

"I know. I just wish he was happy for me."

"He is. He's just scared."

"My father scared? I don't think so, grandma."

"Believe me, the last thing he wants, is to lose you."

"I know he's worried about something happening to me."

"It's not even that. He doesn't want you leaving. I know it's hard for you to see it this way, but you're his little girl and will always be to him."

Nutsy, Kathy, and N-J sit at an outdoor weathered, wooden table at a small clam shack that's a few miles away from the beach. It still looks exactly how it did thirty years ago. N-J buzzes through buttered corn on the cob one after the other, with piles of eaten cobs already on his plate.

"N-J, take it easy," Kathy says.

"She's right. Ya gonna get sick eatin' all this corn."

"I just love this stuff," N-J replies as he takes another bite.

Kathy glances around and says, "This reminds me of the old days coming here after going to the beach."

"Yeah," Nutsy replies while watching N-J enjoy his corn. N-J is having the time of his life and Nutsy couldn't be happier. If only this could be every day, Nutsy thinks.

Carmela and Sammy are still having their conversation together in the kitchen. "Do you have any boyfriends?" Carmela asks.

"Not really."

"You seemed pretty friendly with the boy who was with you at the party."

"Yeah, I don't know. It's confusing right now."

"Relationships can be at times."

"There's more to it than that, grandma."

"Have faith, you'll figure it out." Carmela doesn't press the issue.

"I know what daddy does for a living, but what did he want to be when he was growing up?"

"All I heard about was baseball, baseball, baseball."

"I guess that's where N-J gets it from."

"I still feel so badly for your brother. No one should have to live like that. Was he really that bad living here?"

"Yes, at times. He has the Gento temper."

"I wish he was more like your mother."

"I miss him too when he's not here. It's just not the same."

Squalo and Leo are now wandering through Squalo's apartment checking all the warped floor planks. "These floors are all shot," Leo yells from the dining room.

The doorbell rings and Squalo opens the door. It's the manager of the building and he asks, "Did it dry up yet?"

"Yeah, it's like walking on the Seaside Boardwalk."

"Did you call the insurance company?"

"I'm still waiting for their answer."

"The tenants downstairs want to file it through your policy."

"Suppose they don't cover it?"

"You'll have to pay out of pocket then."

"Fuck that!"

"Well, someone has to."

Leo approaches and says, "Put it through the building's insurance."

"I can't do that."

"Why not? It's a condo, right? Just say the pipe broke." Leo stares the manager down.

The doorbell rings and Squalo says, "It's probably the kid." Squalo moves away.

Leo says to the manager, "I'll just bust a pipe if I have to."

While Squalo opens the door to let Vito in, the manager decides this is a good time to bolt and says, "I'll get back to you."

Leo replies, "Yeah, don't forget."

Vito follows Squalo into the living room and exchanges a handshake with Leo. "Have a seat," Leo says.

They all take a seat and Squalo asks, "So what's the verdict?"

"I'll do it. Maybe I'll even give the wife a shot if she's around," Vito replies with a laugh.

Leo is not thrilled with his answer and asks, "How old are you?"

"Twenty."

"Twenty years old and you still talk like a moron? I don't get these kids today."

Vito replies, "Hey look, I'm not gonna sit here and be insulted by you two."

"Then get the fuck out," Leo replies with a stern look.

Vito hesitantly responds, "I'll see what I can find out. Ya got anything else? I gotta get back to the shop."

Squalo replies, "Yeah, sharpen the fuck up or you'll be back in The Hills in no time."

Vito now races out of the apartment and slams the door shut. He's not thrilled with how they are both treating him.

"I'm not too impressed with this punk so far at all," Leo says.

"They all need time. You did too," Squalo replies.

CHAPTER 25

Later that afternoon, Belinda and Munchie are having an early dinner at Roma's Italian Restaurant on the main avenue, since they have decided not to hide their relationship anymore. Although being out in public is a big step for them, they seem preoccupied with their own thoughts.

Munchie appears like a total mess. His hair's disheveled and his eyes are puffy since he hasn't been able to sleep lately.

Belinda appears troubled since Leo got out. He is the last person she thought she'd have to deal with at this time and is wavering about whether to stay involved or not.

Munchie attempts to spark up a conversation and asks, "How's it going with your brother?"

"Don't ask… I know he's my brother, but I hate the fact he got out."

"I'm sure he'll be on probation for a long time."

Belinda laughs and replies, "Sure, like that means anything to him… he's already taking over the shop."

"Why?"

"That's what my father wants."

"Even after all these years? You did a great job running it."

"They have their own agenda… I'll leave it at that… and I'm not sure I want any part of it anyway."

"What are you going to do then?"

"I'm not sure yet… it's all I've ever known."

It's around five o'clock and Ladro slips on a chest holster and slides a pistol into it. He puts on a jacket and walks out of his bedroom.

Nutsy is in his bedroom and slides on a belt pistol holder on the inside of his pants. He snaps a sleeve into his pistol and slips it into the holster. He puts on a sweater and hangs it over his belt to hide the pistol.

Nutsy is now driving toward a tavern to meet up with Ladro and Squalo. This is the final meeting of his decision and either the continuation of his partnership or a new beginning.

Vito sits in a parked car across the street from Ladro's house. He already noticed Blackie leave and take off in her car. Ladro finally walks out of his house and heads toward his car that's parked on the street.

Vito ducks down to hide his head under the dashboard while Ladro gets into his car and drives off.

Ladro is now heading down the street when his Bluetooth rings and he answers, "Yeah."

Nutsy is currently parking in front of the tavern and asks, "Ya on your way yet?"

"Yeah… shit, I forgot to snap a new clip in. Fuck! I'll be right there."

"Alright, I'll meet ya inside." Nutsy slides out of the car.

Vito has already made his way into Ladro's house through a side door. As Bandit charges over toward him growling and tugs on his pants, Vito violently kicks Bandit away. She flies in the air, smacks against a wall, and crashes onto the wood floor.

Vito snoops around the house searching for the cash. He wanders into the kitchen, opens a closet door and pokes through some boxes.

Nutsy strolls into a private area in the back of the tavern and notices Squalo and Donnola sitting together. Nutsy takes a seat and Squalo asks, "Where's your prick friend? I have a few things to discuss with him."

"Don't worry, he'll be here."

"I ain't worried," Squalo sneers as he gives Nutsy a look. The tension is rising.

So Nutsy sarcastically asks, "How'd ya like the freebie last night?"

"Freebie? It cost us a hundred and eighty-five thousand."

"Not me. Ya better get –"

Leo quickly struts in and pauses while staring Nutsy down with the same intense look he always has. "The king of the hill," Leo sarcastically says.

"I see they're lettin' all the rats out, ha?" Nutsy replies.

Leo laughs and says, "I can see you haven't lost your sense of humor, YET!" Leo's eyes have a piercing glare.

Nutsy can't help but laugh.

"Yeah, keep laughing. That night will catch up to you and The Pope one day, the other fucking bullshit artist."

"Here we go, with this imaginary night again."

Although Squalo loves the bickering, he decides to cut in, "Alright, enough of this bullshit. Let's get down to business."

Ladro roams into his living room and notices Bandit sprawled out on the floor. He squats down to nudge her, but Bandit doesn't move. He thinks she's just sleeping but she's really knocked out from banging her head against the wall.

He hears a creak from the other room and holds steady. He turns his head and hears another creak, so he quietly slips out his pistol.

As Ladro slowly steps into the kitchen, Vito creeps up from behind him. Ladro quickly turns, points the gun and presses the trigger. The trigger only snaps and doesn't fire since the cartridge is empty.

Vito nervously smashes Ladro in the head with a glass that shatters all over the floor. Ladro immediately stumbles backwards, falls, and cracks his head against a chair then crashes onto the ground.

While Ladro lies sprawled out on the ground, Vito nervously bolts away.

Nutsy peeks at his watch while sitting across from the three of them now. He presses a button on his cell phone and impatiently waits for Ladro to answer but the voicemail picks up again.

Squalo says, "You see, he's proving me right. He doesn't wanna show his face." So Squalo slides the rubber shark across to Nutsy and sarcastically says, "Here, I think he lost something."

Nutsy flings the shark toward Squalo's face and replies, "Let's get down to business. I'm gettin' tired of lookin' at your mug."

Leo replies, "You better get used to seeing them since things are gonna change around here."

"I'm sure your probation officer would love to hear this."

Leo laughs and replies, "You know, Nutsy, I know your game. You come across like this loving family man, but you're a criminal at heart. You got everyone fooled, like a fucking hypocrite."

Squalo chimes in, "Whoa, we're here for –"

"Test me, lion, and ya might just find out," Nutsy replies with a serious tone.

"Yeah what? What are you gonna do, take me out and spend the rest of your life behind bars? You already dodged the big one, let's call it what it is."

"I don't get it. Some people are so stuck on the past, they can't see the future."

Leo replies, "Oh, I can. I'm gonna turn that sports park I heard you love into a fucking junkyard. I'll have every crack smoking, needle talking degenerate camping out there. Maybe, I'll even rent tents."

Nutsy just stares. Leo knows he pushed Nutsy's button and gives him a smirk. Squalo's annoyed by Leo's comment and says, "Enough of this bullshit. We ain't here for that dump."

After returning from Sally's Deli, Blackie enters her house and proceeds into the kitchen. She freezes when she notices Ladro sprawled out on the floor and drops her bags. "Ladro!" She squats down and nervously yanks out her cell phone and dials Nutsy.

Nutsy answers his cell phone, "Do you know –"

Blackie frantically cuts him off. "Nutsy, Ladro's on the –"

"Slow down. Slow down."

Blackie gains her composure and says, "Ladro's on the kitchen floor. I think he might be dead."

Nutsy nervously hops up and replies, "Call an ambulance. I'll meet ya at the hospital."

Nutsy stares them all down and says, "I'm out and I'll be expecting my money back... and I better not find out either one of you has anything to do with Ladro." Nutsy storms out.

Squalo and Leo catch eyes since they both think Vito might have something to do with this. So Squalo calls Vito's number as Vito now flies down the street in his car. Vito answers his cell phone and says, "I swear he did it."

"What are you talking about?"

"Ladro. He pulled a gun on me and I got nervous and smashed him with a glass."

Squalo stands up and asks, "Who told you to fucking do that?"

"I swear it wasn't on purpose."

Leo can sense the urgency in Squalo's voice and yanks the phone out of his hand. "Get to the shop now! And don't say a fucking word to anyone!"

CHAPTER 26

Nutsy nervously paces in the emergency room alone since he was right around the corner from the hospital.

Blackie and Kathy charge in. Tears stream down Blackie's cheeks while she hugs Nutsy. "He's unconscious but hanging in thank God," Nutsy says.

As Nutsy and Kathy catch eyes, she turns to wipe a tear. Blackie says, "I swear, Nutsy, when I find out –"

"Take it easy. Let's take –"

"Don't tell me to fucking take it easy! That's my husband God Damnit!"

Patients glance toward Blackie wondering what the ruckus is. She notices and yells out, "What the fuck are you all looking at?" They turn away and go about their business.

Nutsy and Kathy catch eyes again. Kathy gestures to leave it alone right now. She knows Nutsy would just upset Blackie further.

Blackie paces the floor pissed off and upset at the same time. "I kept asking him, what's going on? Nothing, nothing… it's always a fucking secret with you two."

Nutsy glances toward Kathy again. She shakes her head no since she knows this isn't the time for Nutsy to go back and forth with Blackie. It will only stir her up even further, so he remains quiet.

Billy charges in and asks, "Is he okay?"

Nutsy replies, "We're waiting to hear."

It's about an hour later and Leo has Vito tied up to a chair in the back of the body shop and cracks him in the mouth. "You were told to look for cash, that was it."

As blood rolls down Vito's lip, he nervously replies, "I had no choice. He pulled a gun on me."

Leo throws another hard right, striking Vito on the cheek. "Do you know what you just did?"

Squalo says, "Leo, take it easy. He had no choice."

Leo turns toward Squalo and replies, "He should've finished him then. He fucked up twice."

It's about an hour later and everyone is now piled in Ladro's room. He's still unconscious but at least holding steady. Blackie quietly sits in the corner alone. A police officer enters the room and asks, "I need to take a statement, who can give it?"

Nutsy says, "I'll do it."

So Nutsy and the officer step out of the room and walk to a private area down the hallway. "I have to do this, Nutsy."

"It's alright. What do you need?"

"Was anyone home with him?"

"Apparently not?"

"Do you know where he was going?"

"Yeah, he was meeting me at the tavern but forgot something and had to go back home."

"And then what?"

"My sister found him on the floor when she got home about a half an hour later."

"Do you think she had anything –"

"Are you for real?" Nutsy asks with an annoyed stare.

The officer hesitates and replies, "I'm sorry, Nutsy, but I have to ask."

"No, of course not."

"Alright, eventually I'll need to speak with her. This is enough for now. We're all pulling for him."

Nutsy nods and they exchange a handshake. Nutsy roams back into the room and a doctor follows behind him. Everyone stands nervously around the doctor waiting to hear his comments. "He's unconscious right now since he lost a lot of blood. Tomorrow will be an important day for him."

As Blackie breaks down in tears, the doctor turns back and asks, "Has he been in pain at all?"

Nutsy replies, "A little bit with his leg here and there, why?"

"His blood results show a very high level of pain killers and alcohol in it."

"Well, we had a party last night."

The doctor nods and asks, "What about the pain killers?"

Nutsy just shrugs. He has a feeling Ladro loaded up to do the job and doesn't want to commit.

It's about two hours later and only Nutsy and Blackie remain in the room. Blackie just stares at Ladro with a blank look on her face. Nutsy is steaming inside but is trying to hold it together for Blackie at this moment.

"This changes the game, Nutsy."

"Blackie, let's not jump to conclusions yet."

"You know this is all because of what he did, right?"

"Look, maybe it was just a local punk who got scared."

"Sure. What a coincidence."

"Let's be real, if it was more than that, whoever it was, would've finished him right then and there."

"I'm telling you now. All bets are off. I don't give a shit if Leo is around or not."

"Let me hold onto his gun for the time being," Nutsy replies since he's concerned about Blackie having Ladro's pistol.

"Nah, it's alright. I'll hold it."

"I'm picking it up tomorrow." Nutsy doesn't want Blackie doing anything crazy with it.

Blackie doesn't respond ignoring his comment.

"Go home and get some rest. I'll stick around for a little while," Nutsy says.

Blackie nods and stands up. "I have to get back for Bandit anyway. She was sleeping when I left."

It's about a half an hour later and Billy wanders into Ladro's room and asks, "Any changes?"

Nutsy shakes his head no. Billy takes a seat next to Nutsy and glances at Ladro. "I can't believe he's like this."

Nutsy nods but stays silent.

"I'm sorry, Nutsy. I take some blame for this."

"It's not your fault. It is what it is."

"Yeah, in a way it is."

"Look, we don't know who it is yet."

"You're right. I might be jumping the gun... has anyone reached out yet?"

Nutsy shakes his head no.

"How's Blackie?"

"She's beside herself. I'm worried about her."

"She's gonna take this personally, you know that."

"Forget her. I take it personally."

"Take it as it comes. I'll see you in the morning… and go straight home when you leave here." Billy doesn't want Nutsy making any pit stops.

"Oh shit, we have the fundraiser tomorrow afternoon."

"What time is that game on?"

"Four o'clock. Smack in the middle of the cocktail hour."

"Hey look, if you don't wanna go, they'll understand."

"Nah, I do. I wanna look those pricks in the eyes and see what they say."

"You think they'll show up?"

"If they didn't, it would be pretty obvious, wouldn't ya say?"

"True… what about the game?"

"To be honest, Billy, I really don't give a shit anymore. I'm gettin' tired of all this."

"Hang in there." Billy taps Nutsy on the shoulder and heads out of the room.

Nutsy sits alone in thought gazing toward Ladro. He knows Blackie is right and this could change everything. He stands up and paces the floor.

Papo roams in and says, "I heard. I'm sorry, Nutsy."

As they shake hands, Nutsy replies, "Shit, I haven't seen ya in years, and now I see ya twice in one weekend."

They both take a seat and The Pope replies, "I just want you to know, I have your back."

"I don't need the money."

"I'm not talking about that."

So Nutsy glances toward The Pope. He has a feeling where he's heading with this and replies, "That's erased from my mind, Papo. I told ya that already."

"I know… our hands might be forced again."

"Look, we were both young and startin' out. I've paid my price already." Nutsy always felt that his son's situation was payback from the Man above for what he had done that night.

He never discussed this with anyone, not even Kathy but it's a guilt that he's been carrying around for many years. He knows someone had to do it or the city would've been taken over, but always felt his son has paid the ultimate price for it.

"This is an internal problem and must be dealt with that way."

"We don't even know what we're dealin' with right now."

"It doesn't take a rocket scientist to figure this one out… get some sleep. You look tired."

Nutsy and The Pope shake hands. While Papo strolls out, Nutsy can't help but think about Leo's comment and says, "Before ya go, I need to ask ya something."

As Papo turns and nods, Nutsy asks, "You still into baseball?"

"Of course, I got season tickets in the Bronx, why?"

"Do ya think you can build a baseball complex?"

"Where's this coming from?"

"Do ya?"

"I'm sure I can. The question is where?"

"We'll talk another time."

"Get some rest, Nutsy, you're not thinking straight." Papo walks out.

As Nutsy stares at Ladro in thought, his mind drifts back to that night, thirty years ago. The Westerns were having a grand old time in the bowling alley, drinking the booze, and plotting their next moves. They had the city almost in the palm of their hands at that time.

A young Nuccio and Papo stood in the back of the alley holding pistols and Papo said, "We do this right, get out, and never speak about it again, okay?"

Nuccio replied, "This is our time to make things right. No one ever takes over our city."

Papo replied, "You got that fucking right. No one, ever."

Papo stuck his hand out. Nuccio placed his hand on top of Papo's hand and said, "Tonight, we show these Westerns they fucked with the wrong four-square-miles."

"We get one shot to do this right, Nuccio. Make 'em all count."

They slid masks over their faces, snapped cartridges into their pistols, bolted out of the back, and sprayed bullets all over. The Westerns had no shot and were totally caught off guard. They were all wiped out that night.

It's late at night, Squalo and Leo are now leaving the shop after Leo roughed up Vito. Squalo glances at Leo with a pissed off look and says, "This is bullshit… it's your first night out and –"

"If it wasn't me, it would've been someone else with this moron… we couldn't take a chance with Nutsy finding out anyway."

"Who do you think fingers will point to anyway?"

"Let them point all they want… I gotta tell you, it felt good tonight… I think I'm finally back."

"I already had Nutsy backed into a corner. This is the last fucking thing I need."

"You really think I give a shit about Nutsy's decision?"

While Squalo and Leo catch eyes, Squalo notices Leo's intense glare and replies, "Well, apparently not."

"You might've gotten pushed out, but I ate rat food for years while they all soaked in glory… it's my time to shine now."

For once in his life, Squalo wonders if he made the right move letting Leo take back over. Things have been at least calm under Belinda's watch and she is easier to manipulate.

Leo continues, "And let's face it, you ain't living too bad in your high-rise apartment overlooking The Plains."

Squalo ignores Leo's comment and pulls over and parks. "Just fucking hurry up!"

Leo steps out of the car and pops open the trunk. Vito's body is lying face down. Leo lifts him out of the trunk, hurls him over his shoulder and wanders toward an area of woods and thick brush.

Leo tramples through branches and leaves with Vito's limp body hanging over his shoulder.

Leo pauses, lunges forward, and Vito's body flies forward and crashes onto a thick pile of brush. Leo kicks the brush and piles of leaves around to cover Vito's body.

Leo slips back into Squalo's car and asks, "Are you sure this is a good spot?"

Squalo doesn't reply and hits the gas with an annoyed look.

It's early in the morning and Nutsy stands near Ladro's bed. He couldn't sleep well and was hoping to walk in and see Ladro awake, but he's not. Nutsy has been thinking about how things are progressing and if The Pope is correct about Squalo and Leo.

The last thing he would ever want to do is have to get involved in another situation like the past. Nutsy and The Pope made a pact that night for as long as they were both alive, no one or group would ever take over this city that had bad intentions.

Blackie wanders in and asks, "Did you sleep here last night?"

"Nah, I just got here myself." Nutsy hands Blackie a container of coffee and they both quietly take a seat. About a minute goes by while they stare in thought and Nutsy finally says, "I'm sure Bandit misses him."

"I'm taking her to the vet later. She has a lump on her head."

"What happened?"

"I'm not sure. She seems off for some reason."

"She probably ran into something. Ya know how puppies are."

As Blackie shrugs, Nutsy continues, "Look, I've been thinking, I don't want ya involved."

"Too late. I'm already involved whether you like it or not."

"I'm not like Leo. I don't drag my sister into my dirt."

Blackie laughs and replies, "I love you, Nutsy, I do. But our hands are already dirty. We can't change the past."

"True... but we can change the future."

Blackie laughs and replies, "I know what you're doing. You're –"

BEEEEEEEEEEEEP. Ladro flatlines.

Nutsy leaps up and yells, "Nurse!"

A few nurses come charging in. Nutsy and Blackie stand off to the side in shock.

A doctor races in and says, "I need you both to stand outside."

So Nutsy and Blackie nervously race out of the room and pause in the hallway. They are both speechless and in shock at this moment. Blackie wipes tears that stream down her cheek.

"Blackie, don't –"

"Don't say a word to me."

"What did I do?"

"I know Ladro would never do this without your approval. You gave him the nod, didn't you? Even with all this shit going on?"

"Blackie, I –"

"Blackie nothing. I don't even wanna fucking hear it… and let me not get started on the pain killers he probably ate like candy to pull this off."

Nutsy remains quiet. He knows this isn't the place or time to get into it with Blackie considering he doesn't have a leg to stand on. So Nutsy just sighs. He feels the weight of the world on his shoulders right now.